Kill the Crazy

Madison Cruz Mystery 2

Lucy Carol

Copyright © 2014 Fevered Publishing LLC 2nd Edition
Print Edition

ISBN: 978-0-9896735-5-6

Fevered Publishing LLC
19410 Highyway 99, Suite A-234
Lynnwood, WA 98036

Website
LucyCarol.com

Facebook
www.facebook.com/lucycarolbooks

Email
lucy@lucycarol.com

All rights reserved. No part of this publication may be reproduced, distributed or transmitted in any form or by any means, or stored in a database or retrieval system, without the prior written permission of the publisher.

Dedication

To my favorite superhero Irrational Man for understanding my irrational need for fresh flowers next to my laptop, especially in the dreary dead of winter.

About This Book

In a tranquil spa for the wealthy, candlelit massages, waterfall pools, and flowing wine should add up to the ultimate relaxing day. But Madison Cruz soon finds hidden agendas and danger. A catacomb of hallways and a tangled web of motives hints at madness beneath the sophisticated veneer of the spa. Meanwhile, Madison's FBI mother and KGB grandmother are still learning how to get along after trying to outshoot each other. As if that weren't enough, now Jason's evil ex-girlfriend thinks Madison stole her man, and the wine is flying! Hiding out in the supply room isn't helping—not with Jason trying to help himself to Madison's charms. As much as she'd like to return his attentions, she'd better stay alert to the danger just outside their door. Things are about to go from dangerous… to deadly.

Chapter One

MADISON TRIED TO be a good girl, damn it. She told herself to go along with it: don't complain, don't spoil everyone's fun, don't tell everyone they were all going to die.

As their enclosed gondola rounded to the top of the giant Ferris wheel, she convinced herself that she was pulling it off; that no one knew about her panic. As long as she kept her eyes away from the four glass walls surrounding them, resisting the urge to look down at the ground, she'd be fine. Thank God the floor wasn't glass too.

There was a nice paycheck at the end of this gig, although she'd have to give Phil a piece of her mind when it was over. He knew damn well she had a fear of heights, but he had let her think the photo shoot would take place in the restaurant at the foot of the Ferris wheel. She'd like to think her agent would look out for her sanity as well as her employment, but she wasn't too surprised. Phil would book his own grandmother for a dog fight if the price were right.

The costume she wore was a Blue Heron, Seattle's official bird. It was her job to pose for publicity pictures with Iris Alexander, the wealthy owner of the soon-to-be-built Blue Heron Mall. Iris's sleek brown hair reflected the sunlight as they sat together, glass wall behind them. A sweep of high-rise buildings filled the background. The morning sun ignited the dazzle of the city.

"Hey, bird person," said an irritated voice, breaking Madison's concentration. She looked up at the thin, blond photographer as he lowered his camera. With a big sigh he said, "Would you please stop staring at the floor?"

She took a deep breath and fixed her eyes on him, trying to ignore the glass walls in her peripheral vision.

"That's right. Look at me. Let us see those pretty green eyes." He aimed the camera, his voice taking on a cheerful quality. "You and the client person… celebrating… you're so happy…"

Madison concentrated. *Look at the camera, look at the camera…*

"Okay, now you're a deer in the headlights," he said, rubbing his face.

"I'm sorry," she said, panicking for new reasons. A big paycheck was at stake here, so she had to get a grip. *Think of the money, think of the money.*

"I'm happy now, see?" She put on her most dazzling smile. "Celebrating…" As she turned her head to show the client her gorgeous smile, she smacked Iris's forehead with the long skinny beak. "Oh! Sorry, Iris!"

With a subtle jerk of her head, Iris remained composed, leaning away from Madison to smooth down her hair, its shoulder length cut falling perfectly back into place. She smiled politely and motioned to her nearby assistant. "A little help here?"

The assistant stood up to a partially bent position, her flawless skin and deep ruby lips suggesting her attention to detail. The gondola was not tall enough to stand fully upright in, unless a person was under five foot four, which the assistant clearly was not. She came forward to check Iris's perfect hair, pretending to fix something. With a sharp glance at Madison, the assistant's gray eyes conveyed disapproval. Then stepping back to her seat next to the photographer, she scribbled a note on a clipboard.

Madison wondered if those notes were about her. She felt tattled on.

Dramatic sighs came from the photographer. "We only have a few more minutes before they start to rotate the wheel again," he said, looking at Madison. "Please don't make me lose my shot."

"Troy dear, I'm not worried," said Iris, leaning back in, close to Madison. "You always manage to pull off miracles."

He smiled. "That's why you're my favorite client person. You have faith in me."

"And it helps that she rented the entire wheel," said Madison in a sunny voice, "so our gondola can stay at the top."

All three turned to look at her in silence. She gently flapped her wings on her thighs, noting how difficult it was to maintain credibility when you're dressed like a bird. "I was just saying how lucky we are," she added.

The assistant looked down and scribbled another note.

Madison could feel the headpiece of her costume coming loose, causing the beak to droop. But with feathers for hands she needed help to fix it.

"Okay, let's try this again," said Troy.

"Um, could I get some help from the assistant person?" she asked. "My head piece is getting wobbly."

"Excuse me?" The assistant's face went hard. "I have a name. It's Catherine Gabrielle."

Madison's headpiece continued to fall forward. She pushed it back up with her feathered appendage. "I'm sorry Catherine, I didn't mean—"

"Ca-ther-ine Ga-bri-elle," she said slowly, looking Madison in the eye. There seemed to be an expectation, so Madison repeated the name while the assistant joined in unison.

"Ca-ther-ine Ga-bri-elle," they said.

More sighs from Troy. "Client person, while they're working this out, would you scoot forward in your seat, please?" he asked pleasantly. "That's it. Big pretty smile. When the bird person is ready, we'll have her leaning over right behind you. Those blue feathers will make your eyes pop."

Madison shoved her headpiece back up, harder this time. "Never mind about the head piece," she said in resignation. "This is fine." She leaned behind Iris, trying not to look at the window, not look at the floor, not be a deer in the headlights. Instead she focused on pleasant thoughts. *Plot Phil's demise, plot Phil's demise...*

"Bird person, turn your head to a profile behind Iris's head... no... please don't shut your eyes... come on. That's it. Now tilt your beak upward so that—"

Suddenly the gondola vibrated as the giant Ferris wheel began to turn again. Madison jumped, throwing her winged arms up with a scream, propelling herself away from the glass and into Iris and the photographer.

The assistant took a note.

✧ ✧ ✧

"PHIL, YOU DON'T understand," said Madison into her cell phone. "They'd have nothing to complain about if you hadn't booked me for a photo shoot in a glass cage, 175 feet up in the air!"

She threw her tote bag onto her bed and pulled the hairband from her ponytail. Her shiny dark hair spilled over her shoulders while she tried to rub the tension out of her head with one hand.

"You should be grateful," he said in his Boston street accent. "That was a fantastic gig for you. I'm always looking out for my little Chocolate Mint." Phil often likened her pale green eyes, fringed with black lashes, to chocolate mints.

"Don't 'Chocolate Mint' me," she said. "I was terrified. Afterward, I couldn't stop apologizing to Iris."

"And here I thought the scariest part would be working with Iris Alexander herself," said Phil. "You could get pointers on how to eat your rival for lunch from what I hear."

"At least she was the nicest of the three of them," said Madison. She dug around inside her tote bag looking for the gift envelope that Nika, her new Russian grandmother, had given her.

"Well she plays hardball in all her business interests, I'll tell you that," said Phil. "Having money ain't enough for her. Iris likes to win."

Madison sighed. "I can't imagine what it's like to not worry about money."

"Which is why I get you good gigs."

"And why I do them even if they're up in the air. But have a heart next time, will you, Phil? You know I have a hard time with heights."

"Yeah? Well, how about paychecks? You have a hard time with those too? That's going to be a big one, you know. Jen almost killed me when I gave the job to you instead of her."

"Well maybe you should've given it to her. Then you wouldn't be getting complaints from Ca-ther-ine Ga-bri-elle."

She found the envelope and exhaled in relief. It held the potential to make this all go away. It was a day pass for two people to a luxury spa. She and her girlfriend Spenser had been invited to meet up with Nika and Madison's mother, Ann, for a special afternoon of pampering.

"You kidding?" said Phil. "I can't trust Jen with classy clients, you know that. The complaints would've been about being trapped in that glass cage with a naked maniac."

"You might have a point," said Madison.

"You know Jen. There's no gig that she thinks can't be made better by taking everything off."

"Phil, I'm just saying that I can't do my best work when I'm scared."

"Come on, Minty," his voice softened, "I knew it'd be a little tough for you, but I also knew that you always pull through, girl. And this time is no exception."

"How can you say that? The assistant called you and ratted me out. They may withhold payment over this."

"I say it because Troy called me after I hung up with the assistant, and he's thrilled. They don't dare withhold payment if they want to use that shot."

"I don't get it," said Madison. "What shot? The whole thing was a screw up."

"That last shot was the money shot, Minty. He loves it. Iris Alexander loves it."

"The last… what?" She sat down on the bed.

"He said it was an action shot, that you were freakin' out, throwing your arms up or something. But it looked like the Blue Heron opened its wings like the stupid bird is blessing Iris or some garbage, and they can see the head piece and beak, but your scream was hidden behind Iris's head, her beaming smile, blah blah blah." He took a breath. "Doesn't matter. They're *happy*, you understand? You'll be seeing that shot all over Seattle. They're even buying bus ads. How do you like that, eh? My little Minty on a bus."

"It *worked out?*" She couldn't believe it.

"Sure did. But now I gotta find extra gigs for Jen to make it up to her or she'll make my life hell after what happened at her gig."

"I'm afraid to ask."

"She was hoping you'd chicken out at the last minute on account of the height and all that, so she made changes to her costume to look like a Blue Heron."

"How can a stripper look like a Blue Heron?"

"She put lots of blue feathers in key places, if you know what I mean. Assumed she could rush over to the Blue Heron gig and be a sexy little birdie or something. But she used the wrong glue for that sort of thing and those feathers wouldn't come off during her dance without a lot of yanking and cursing."

After hanging up, Madison got ready for the spa. The morning's gig was behind her now, and she could let herself relax a little, maybe get some of that tension out of her shoulders. She tried to let the good news sink in that the photo shoot wasn't as disastrous as she'd thought. The shot would even be used as a bus ad, although no one would be able to tell it was Madison. She pursed her lips as she gave that some thought.

Looking at the clock she noted it was almost time to make the obligatory scream call. After all, Spenser and she were about to be partaking of the most talked about luxury spa in Seattle, The Lazy Petal. She had to hurry.

She changed her clothes and packed her bag for the spa, hoping she could afford a massage. As she thought about the bus ad, she decided she was glad no one would recognize her since she didn't want to tell her mom about it anyway. They were getting along better than they ever had, and she didn't want to ruin it by reminding her mother of the main thing she still disapproved of: Madison's job.

She was eager to see if her mother and Nika were getting along better than the last time she'd seen them together, which was at a gun range. Her mom had finally come to accept the truth about Nika as her own biological mother, and had invited her to some target practice. This seemed like an odd getting-to-know-you outing, but as uncomfortable as Madison was around guns, she couldn't resist the invitation to come along.

No doubt about it, the shock of how Nika entered their lives had thrown a new light on everything. Watching her mother take tentative steps toward forming a relationship with Nika made Madison proud of her. Ann may have spent her days fighting crime as an FBI Special Agent, but this was the bravest thing Madison had ever seen her do.

Her cell phone doodled a happy tune. Darn it, Spenser beat her to it. She picked up her phone, hit the answer button and put the phone to her ear. Silence. She waited the customary two seconds because she-who-makes-the-call gets to scream first. Spenser screamed into the phone and Madison screamed back and hung up. At twenty-four years old they still hadn't grown tired of this little ritual left over from their high school days.

She was glad that Spenser would be there to share in all the fun. It made Madison happy that Ann was giving Nika a chance, but they needed more time, and the spa was as good a place as any for everyone to continue getting to know each other.

What could possibly go wrong?

Chapter Two

"OH MY GOD, Spenser. It's him," Madison whispered. "Stay in line, and don't move." Her breathy whisper had panic in it.

Madison ducked behind Spenser as the spa manager in black uniform passed the line of women at the check-in counter.

"What, the manager?" whispered Spenser. "Why?"

"Act natural," said Madison. "I swear it's him."

"Him who?" whispered Spenser.

"The guy."

"What guy?"

"You're not acting natural."

"Me? What about you?"

"I'm not supposed to be acting natural," said Madison as she hid her face behind Spenser's blond hair. "I'm hiding, for God's sake."

"What guy, damn it?" said Spenser.

"The guy I buried alive."

"Oh." Spenser blinked, as the thought seemed to sink in. "So… you think he's still mad?"

In the posh front lobby, the line moved forward, bringing Madison and Spenser closer to the check-in counter. Black uniformed clerks with pleasant smiles greeted each patron, the plastic clacking of keyboards filling the room as they checked them in.

Stepping behind the counter, the dark haired manager mumbled to a lady in black uniform. Her neat ponytail swept across her shoulder as she turned her head toward him.

"Clare, in case I don't see Lettie," said the manager, "could you remind her I need to leave for a dental appointment this afternoon?" Looking grim, he walked away.

"It's safe," said Spenser. "He's gone. Reminds me of a cute college professor I had."

Madison came out from behind Spenser and snapped her fingers, remembering. "Frank Bergman. That was his name."

"Don't say 'was' as if he died. He's not the dearly departed."

"No. He's the pissed and present."

"It was an accident, Madison. It could happen to anybody."

Madison looked her in the eye, making her point with her silence.

"Okay, you're right," said Spenser. "This stuff only happens to you. But still, it was an accident. The prop malfunctioned."

"The crew tried to explain it to him but he wouldn't listen."

"Kind of hard to listen when you're traumatized. But that was, what… two years ago?"

Madison looked around, her eyes full of concern. "If he sees me, don't say anything about Mom and Nika in front of him. I don't want him to involve them."

"Come on," said Spenser, pushing Madison's dark hair back behind her shoulders. "You're making a big deal out of nothing."

"Well I did, you know, sort of bury him and stuff."

"Well, yeah, there's that."

"Surely he has lots of administrative things to do in his office?" said Madison, trying to encourage herself.

"And while he's in his office we'll all be getting pampered in The Lazy Petal," said Spenser, gently shaking Madison's shoulders.

Madison's smile slowly returned. Coming to the front of the line, she handed the day pass to a clerk whose name badge read Clare. Clare smiled and entered their information in the computer. Looking at her screen, she asked, "Are you Madison Cruz?"

"Yes."

Her brow creased. She typed some more and stared. "I'm sorry. I should probably get the manager to help me."

"I'd rather not bother him," said Madison, trying to think fast. "It's just a day pass from my grandmother. If it's expired I'll pay for it myself." She felt Spenser squeeze her arm. They both knew how expensive that would be.

"Quite the opposite," said Clare. "There's a new account set up for you. All services are available to you every day, and all charges are waived." She put her fingertips to her cheek. "I've never seen one like this." She looked up at Madison. "Please forgive me for not knowing who you are."

Madison's face felt stuck. She finally managed to say, "What?"

"Are you an actress?" said Clare.

"Well, I… was a bird this morning."

An older woman with perfect makeup and gray streaked hair in a stylish bob appeared behind the counter and looked over Clare's shoulder. "Well, what have we here?" Her eyes lit up with interest as she scanned the screen. Her name tag on her black uniform jacket read, Lettie, Assistant Manager.

"Thank goodness you're here," said Clare. "None of the usual codes are working. I've never seen an account like this."

Clare stepped back as Lettie took over. She typed with impeccable nails, her eyes scanning the screen. "Who set this up for you, dear?" She looked at Madison.

"I don't know. There must be some mistake," said Madison. "My grandmother gave me a day pass for two. That's all."

"Your grandmother's name?"

"Veronica Fedora." Lettie typed as Madison spoke. "We call her Nika. She has a permanent day pass and can bring visitors if she likes."

Lettie scanned the screen. "Yes, I see that here. And now it's been extended to you. Curious." She looked at Madison. "Your grandmother has no address."

Madison had no answer for her. What would be safe to say? She wanted to wrap her arms around herself, but resisted.

"Is she friends with the owner?" asked Lettie.

"I don't know," said Madison, her discomfort growing. "She said it was an added thank you for work she did for the owner." She almost wished Frank Bergman would come out and make a fuss. Anything to change this subject.

Lettie held her gaze on Madison for a moment, her expression neither approving nor disapproving. Finally she said, "Such privilege is rare around here."

Lettie turned to Clare. "Frank must have set it up. You'll need to use the VIP code to check them in."

"I thought that code was only reserved for the owner, or her family," said Clare.

"Yes," said Lettie. "It was." She returned her gaze to Madison. "What does your grandmother do?"

Answering Lettie's question made her nervous. Nika was ex-KGB, and Madison wasn't comfortable trying to describe the employment Nika had turned to after the KGB was shut down years ago. It could be called private investigating at best, mercenary spy work at worst. Had Nika and Ann had that talk yet? She'd like to be a fly on the wall for that one.

"Dance teacher," Madison blurted out. "She's a dance teacher." *Oh that's just brilliant Madison. Stupid, stupid...*

"Really?" said Lettie, looking confused.

"Um, yeah, she really knows how to do a good shuffle ball-change."

Lettie and Clare both stared at her. Even Spenser was staring at her. Anxious to get out of there, Madison asked, "So, is everything okay now?"

"Certainly," said Lettie, shaking it off and entering the correct code for a VIP account.

She turned a cool smile their way. "Welcome to The Lazy Petal."

✧ ✧ ✧

"I SHOULD BE thrilled. I should be happy. So why am I nervous instead?" Madison closed the door to her locker, having changed out of her street clothes and into the required spa robe and hair towel. The front check-in lobby led straight into the locker room, so they hadn't actually seen the main spa area yet. Spenser was still neatly folding everything and putting it in her locker, arranging her belongings into some kind of order that to Madison, as usual, seemed like overkill. But she knew Spenser was more peaceful when everything was neat and tidy.

"I think it's because of the way that older lady acted, as if the day pass were suspicious. She should've been happy for you. I don't know. It did feel odd."

"I keep thinking there's some kind of mistake and I'll accidentally run up a bill that's bigger than my rent."

"In this place, that's not hard to imagine, but you should talk to your grandmother. Let her assure you that everything's okay," said Spenser. "Besides, she must have danced pretty hard for this." Her eyes held laughter in them like she could barely contain herself, and in a very unladylike manner, she snorted, falling into giggles.

Madison rolled her eyes. "I had to say *something* about what she does. That was the first thing that entered my head."

"And what are you going to do about Frank?"

"What do you mean?"

"Well she said Frank must have set up your account. If he did, then he knows you're here. If he didn't, then… well…" Spenser trailed off.

"It's all right," said Madison. "You can say it."

"If he didn't, that would only leave Nika, right? And she probably knows how to do stuff like that, right?"

Madison was quiet for a moment. "We don't really know her very well, yet. That's true. But she wouldn't risk causing trouble over something as stupid as a spa pass. So you're probably right about Frank." She didn't know what else she could do but ride out the day. If she ran into Frank, she hoped he would be cordial, and who knows, he might even let her explain that awful day.

Minutes later they left the locker room for the main hallway, stepping out barefooted onto a floor with threads of red embedded in pale marble tiles.

"Holy mackerel," said Madison, coming to a stop in the doorway. The door swung closed, gently hitting her backside like a push of encouragement. "This hallway is wider than my bedroom."

"Everything is wider than your bedroom."

Recessed lighting hidden along the edges of high ceilings threw a soft glow on the walls.

"Look at this place," said Spenser, turning in a circle, her eyes sparkling.

"Take it easy, Spensy. You might hit critical mass and implode."

"I'll die happy."

"But I would miss you," said Madison. "Should I throw down some trash and break the spell?"

"You do, and I'll shoot you."

"No you won't. That would get blood on the pretty floor."

"It's gorgeous." Spenser looked down at the marble tiles. "Looks like streaks of raspberry puree swirled on a frothy cream."

They sighed.

"I feel guilty walking on it," said Spenser.

"I want to eat it," said Madison.

"I think I could still shoot you. Blood coordinates with raspberry. You could get shot in here and match the decor."

"Wow," said Madison. "They thought of everything."

Soft harp music followed them down the hallway, reminding Madison of glass slippers and fairytales. Barefooted ladies passed by in identical robes and hair towels, some of them carrying glasses of wine, some of them with creams or mud on their faces.

On the left side of the hallway was a wall made of rounded gray stones on the bottom half, while the upper half was glass, covered in fluffy white curtains so sheer Madison could see through them to golden points of candlelight that shimmered next to the deep blue of the pools. It was like seeing heaven through a white fog.

In a breathy voice, Spenser said. "It's like a dream. How do you get in there?"

"I'm not sure. I think we're on the south end right now, but this hallway is supposed to run along the south and east sides of the pool room, so I guess we'll come to the entryway if we keep walking."

"But that's huge. Look how far the hallway stretches," said Spenser. "Why would they need a pool that large?"

"It's not one pool, it's four. All free of chemicals, can you believe it? And each pool is a different temperature depending on your preference."

Spenser knit her brows. "But how can that work? The chemicals I mean, how do they keep it clean?"

"The brochure said something about copper and silver ions." Madison shrugged. "I don't understand it, but wouldn't it be cool to go swimming without our eyes getting red?" She looked to the right side of the hallway where all the doors to all the specialty salons were. "There's the nail salon. We're too early for our appointments, but let's go see it."

"You go ahead," said Spenser, "I want to go touch the curtains and see if they're made of polyester."

As Madison approached the nail salon, a pretty young woman in black uniform and honey brown hair changed old flowers for fresh ones on a table near the door. Madison turned to call Spenser when she heard a loud pop of pottery hitting the floor and the clink and clatter of pieces scattering. The young woman who had knocked over the vase stood staring at the flowers and the broken pieces of vase. Some of the shards had skittered across the hallway to where Madison stood.

Madison quickly crouched down to pick up the pieces, moving around the floor to wherever she spied another piece, afraid that someone might come along and step on them. Carefully kneeling, she was filling her palm with several small pieces when Lettie the assistant manager emerged from the nail salon and stood in the doorway. Her icy gaze at the young woman did not look happy.

"Brittany," she said, quiet and exasperated as if in a secret rage. "Now what?"

"Why didn't you tell me he was quitting?" said Brittany, petulant, ignoring the broken vase.

Lettie's voice grew frosty. "Is that what this is about? I've run interference with Frank to clear the way for you, and you're willing to gamble the job for a snit fit?"

"I do want the job, it's just that—"

"If you can't stay off Frank's radar—"

With the pieces of broken pottery in her hand, Madison stepped up, interrupting Lettie. "I'm so clumsy, please forgive me," she said, placing the pieces on the table. "I just wanted to smell the flowers."

"Oh—" said Lettie. She seemed surprised, looking quickly at Brittany and back to Madison. "Please don't worry yourself." She smiled. "Brittany will clean it up. Continue enjoying your stay with us, and don't give it another thought." To Brittany she gave a tight smile. "I'm sorry, dear. I thought you'd broken another one. Resume your duties." She turned to leave, but looked back for a moment, silent. She walked down the hallway, rounded a corner and disappeared.

Brittany looked at Madison with confusion. "Why did you do that?"

"It sounded like you were about to lose your job over a broken vase," said Madison. "I couldn't let that happen."

Expecting a thank-you, she was startled when Brittany spit out, "That was an expensive vase. Maybe I was trying to break it. Maybe I'm tired of the shit I have to put up with around here. Did you ever think of that?"

Not sure how to respond, Madison could only stare in disbelief before answering. "I… no. That thought never crossed my mind."

"I hate this place," said Brittany.

Embarrassed that she'd somehow screwed up, Madison still couldn't understand such a contemptuous response. "I'm sorry I said anything. I was only trying to help."

As Spenser walked up, Brittany said, "Things are not what they seem around here. You should stay out of it."

Without another word the girl left through the doorway into the nail salon.

"What the hell was that?" Spenser asked.

"Good question," said Madison, confused.

"Another glorious welcome to The Lazy Petal?"

"More like red flags. Some people leave big hints that you should stay away from them."

Knowing they had manicures and pedicures scheduled for later, Madison couldn't help but hope that Brittany would be gone by then.

"Forget her," said Spenser. "Let's go find the massage rooms. We have appointments."

"Just promise me no more challenging people to deal with," said Madison. "I think I've met my quota for today."

"That's a good way to look at it. You've met your quota. Everything will be smooth going from here on out."

"Oh man. You had to say that."

Chapter Three

"FIRST, MOM SHOT out his eyes and nose," said Madison. "Then Nika shot a smiley face over his heart. It all happened in seconds."

Lying face down on a massage table, Madison had more to tell Spenser about what happened at the gun range, but instead she took a moment to let herself swoon into the embrace of mud imported from God knows where, full of minerals and magic. *I swear my masseuse just leveled up to angelic status.*

From the next table Spenser said, "Wow. Would I sound twelve years old if I said 'That is so cool'?"

"Yes."

"I don't care. *That is so cool!*"

Within their private room, dozens of little white candle flames danced in the dark, like dreams of pearls and tiny stars, filling the room with a peaceful glow. Two lady masseuses in black uniforms slathered them up and rubbed them down, chasing away all the cares and worries of the previous week.

"It started out as casual target practice, but Mom got fancy on the paper man target, so Nika did too. It turned into a competition of whose dead shot was the deadliest," said Madison. "That paper-man target became bullet art."

"And here you thought your mom wasn't creative," said Spenser.

Friends since childhood, Madison and Spenser had experienced many things together, but never anything like this. They wore only white towels draped over their derrieres, and towels wrapped on their heads. Spenser's blond hair was neatly tucked up and perfect, while Madison's dark hair peeked out around the sides.

Madison closed her eyes, giving in to the angel hands. She murmured, "It gets better. They kept shooting and connected all the holes into a lacy pattern. It's like they were reading each other's minds."

"Deadly but decorative," said Spenser in a muffled voice.

"You should've seen it," said Madison. "Eventually it couldn't hold up under its own weight and tore along those perforated lines. Paper man down." She opened her eyes, pausing in thought. "My new grandmother is so much like my mom it's scary."

"Well," said Spenser, "there is a biological link, after all."

"I have a biological link, too," Madison insisted. "But that was way out of my comfort zone."

Spenser yawned. "Sounds like they're getting to know each other."

"Bonding over bullets."

"Nothing wrong with that."

Madison hesitated, and then said, "I guess not." Thinking about the impromptu contest between her mother and Nika, she wondered if old rivalries between the FBI and the now defunct KGB had anything to do with it. Regardless, it didn't seem quite appropriate for Ann to try to outshoot her own mother. Not that Nika seemed to mind.

Both masseuses began the cleanup, tipping pitchers of herb-infused water to splash over the muddy backs and legs of both Madison and Spenser, wiping them down and pouring more water, removing every last trace of the mud. The delicate splash and drip onto the floor made its own kind of music as the water gently ran, flowing toward a concealed drain. Mild goose bumps played on the surfaces of their skin.

"What about you?" Spenser asked. "I realize your skill wouldn't be like theirs, but how did you do in their contest? How was your aim?"

"Amazing. I was shocked."

"Really?" Spenser turned her head toward her.

"Yeah. I never knew I would be that bad. I swear, I would lose to a dog. I would lose to a box."

Spenser shook with laughter under the splashing water. "You can't be that bad."

"I'd probably do better if I kept my eyes open when I pulled the trigger."

"You closed your eyes?"

Madison looked at her. "I couldn't help it. My whole body jumped at every loud bang."

"Good thing you're not in the spy business," said Spenser.

"I'll leave that to Mom and Nika and stick to acting and singing telegrams, thank you."

"And occasional photo shoots dressed as a bird."

"You just had to remind me. Thanks."

"At least you don't have to worry about guns," said Spenser.

"Nope." Madison exhaled. "Only malfunctioning props or plunging to my death from a Ferris wheel."

The masseuses rubbed down their wet backs and legs with heated towels then added a warm oil, working it in, releasing a subtle scent of cherry blossoms.

"So," said Spenser. "What's the verdict on the new guy? Jason?"

Relishing the cherry blossom scent, Madison pictured petals floating to the ground. "There's no verdict. It's only been a few weeks."

"And?"

"Well, we've only gone out a few times. But he just looks at me and I start to melt."

"Mmm," said Spenser. "Hot item?"

Staring at one of the candle flames, Madison smiled. "Oh yes. Makes it hard to think straight," she admitted. "He works a lot, always has some odd job going on the side, seems more conservative than I'm used to, and he thinks I'm this crazy force of nature."

"You are a crazy force of nature."

"No I'm not. I'm just... restless, sometimes. But the main problem I see with him is his attitude toward *my* job. He doesn't understand why I'm still a small time actress, like if I'm not famous I should quit. He doesn't understand that I like it this way." She sighed and turned her head to the other side. "For now, anyway."

All finished and wrapped in their warm robes, they were each presented with a small complimentary jar of mud to take home. Delighted with their prizes, they put the jars into the deep pockets of their robes.

Returning to the hallway, Madison said, "All right, we're supposed to meet them at the waxing salon." She looked up and down the hallway. "I'm guessing if we keep the white curtains on our left, we'll come to the waxing salon on our right."

"Sounds good," said Spenser. They joined the tranquil traffic of women walking up and down the lovely hallway, coming and going from the various salon doors.

As they passed what appeared to be the facials room, Madison heard familiar voices.

She looked over to the wall by the salon door. Her eyes widened when she saw Iris Alexander. It was one thing to know that the shoot turned out all right this morning, but for Madison it was humiliating to know that the good shot was an accident. Or as Iris might put it, Troy was once again working miracles. She quickly turned her head in the opposite direction so she was facing Spenser.

"What is it?" Spenser asked.

"It's Iris Alexander," she said quietly. "Can you believe my luck today?"

"Well it *is* a high-end luxury spa. She's probably a regular," said Spenser, then added a humph. "Here comes that assistant manager."

Hoping not to be noticed, Madison looked away but could hear the ladies' greetings.

"Lettie," said Iris.

"Iris," Lettie replied, her tone cool and unemotional.

"Keep walking," said Madison in a quiet voice, "nice and casual."

"Don't worry. We're just another couple of towel heads to them," said Spenser.

Madison directed her gaze toward the white curtains of the pool's glass wall while Spenser watched the exchange of the women over Madison's shoulder. Iris's words floated in.

"Frank tells me you're dealing with a certain trouble maker," said Iris.

"Careful, she's nearby," said Lettie.

Madison gasped.

"Shh…" said Spenser.

"You should have seen her this morning," said Iris. "Poor Frank, this must be hard for him. Shouldn't you assign her an escort?"

Lettie's words grew faint as Madison and Spenser kept walking, getting further away. "We prefer the illusion of freedom. No worries. She's being watched and…"

Spenser's lips barely moved as she whispered, "Madison, what's going on? I don't understand."

"Neither do I. If Frank is telling the whole world what a terrible person I am, he's got a bigger problem than I thought. And how did Iris know I was coming here today? Why would anybody care?"

"You know what?" said Spenser as she put her arm around Madison, guiding her toward the waxing salon. "We didn't come here for them. We came here to spend time with your awesome mom, your cool new grandmother, and each other. And I'm pretty fabulous if I say so myself." One corner of Madison's mouth started to lift upward. "Ignore the rich old biddies. You have a

VIP account whether they like it or not, and we don't need them in order to have a wonderful time. You hear me?"

Madison nodded. She was afraid if she spoke she might get teary. She felt stupid that she would let something so dumb get to her. Spenser was right. She was here to spend some relaxing time with her family and best friend.

As she saw the door to the waxing salon get closer, up ahead a woman coming from the wine bar called out her name. "Madison?"

Her glamorous fifty-four year old grandmother Nika, wearing the identical robe and hair towel, came in for a bear hug, holding a glass of red wine in her right hand.

"Nika!" greeted Madison.

In a mild Russian accent, Nika said, "I was not sure it was you. We all look alike in these robes."

With her arms around her grandmother, Madison could see strands of dark red hair escaping the confines of the towel and trailing down her neck.

She disengaged from the hug, turning to Spenser. Spenser held out her hand to shake, but Nika moved in for another bear hug.

"It's an honor meeting you," said Spenser as they broke the hug. "Thank you for inviting me."

"You are welcome, Madison's good friend." Nika looked at Madison. "The word is 'bestie,' yes?

"Yes," said Madison. "It's American slang for best friend."

"My granddaughter's bestie is good to meet," Nika smiled.

"Wow," said Spenser as she looked into Nika's face. She did a double take between her best friend and the older Russian woman. "You weren't kidding. She looks a lot like you. Which makes her gorgeous, of course."

"I like you more and more," said Nika.

"I need to ask you about the day pass," said Madison. "They said an account was set up for me—that there would be no charge for any services."

"And you may come any day," said Nika. "Did they tell you that?"

"You mean… you mean it's true?"

"Of course is true. You and Ann are family now, so you each have account."

Madison hadn't dared to let herself believe it till now. "I don't know what to say!"

Nika took Madison's hand and squeezed it. "You like this, yes?"

"Yes! Thank you." She squeezed back.

Spenser nudged Madison with her elbow. "Tell her the rest," she said, starting to giggle again.

She hated to ruin the moment, but she knew she should tell Nika. "I think the assistant manager wanted to know what you did for the owner to get such privilege, so she asked me what you do. I'm afraid I said a dumb thing."

"In this case, I caught thief and stopped him from selling business secrets. It would've been devastating blow to owner. But," Nika's smile was cavalier, "I do not know this assistant manager. She is not family," she looked over to Spenser, "or bestie. So when people are nosy, I prefer mystery. It tortures them."

"Mystery would've been better," said Madison.

"What is this dumb thing you said?" said Nika.

"I told her you were a dance teacher."

With a gasp, Nika's eyes widened.

"I'm sorry, Nika," said Madison. "I should've clammed up. It's none of her business."

"I love it! Dance teacher. What wonderful thing to be." She looked off in the distance, lost in thought for a moment. "Dance teacher," she murmured. "Come," she said, putting an arm around them both. "Ann is waiting for me to get back from wine bar." She told Spenser, "I think Madison will like wine service in there."

✧ ✧ ✧

SITTING NEXT TO Madison and Spenser on the plush couches of the waxing salon, Nika leaned in and said, "Then Ann told me she's never been waxed before."

"Huh," said Madison. "Well lots of women never—"

"So I scheduled a bikini wax for her."

"Wait. Shouldn't she start with something easier, like brow waxing?"

"She will like result," said Nika.

"But..." Madison didn't quite know how to say it. "If she's never had any kind of waxing done, she won't know what a bikini wax feels like. The first time can be a shock."

A startled squeal from within an adjacent room confirmed it was too late to warn her mother.

In a matter-of-fact tone, Nika said, "She knows now."

Madison and Spenser winced.

"Ann is strong woman," said Nika. "I am certain that next one won't be so loud."

"The next one?" asked Madison.

"Yes. They must do other side."

A much quieter yelp came from the same room. A moment later as the door opened, they all grabbed magazines, looking busy. Ann emerged from the room, clutching her wine glass, her dark eyes stunned. Without a word she walked up to the three of them, took Madison's magazine which was upside down, turned it right side up, and handed it back to her.

She threw back the rest of her wine, swallowing hard, and turned to Nika. In a plaintive voice, she asked, "Why?"

"For your love life," said Nika.

"I just went through that for my love life? I don't *have* a love life."

"We will find you right kind of man," said Nika. "Remember?"

"But," Ann looked uncomfortable, "I thought we were only talking about Madison."

Madison sat up at attention. "What?"

"Madison, I can see," said Ann, gesturing toward her daughter. "But me?"

"See what?" said Madison, looking back and forth between them.

"You are only forty years," said Nika, "You should have sexy life."

"I think they're plotting my future," said Madison.

"My life is just fine," said Ann. "A little complicated at times, especially *now*," she paused. "But overall I like my life the way it is."

Madison looked at Spenser. "Don't just sit there. Hide me."

"No way," said Spenser. "They can shoot smiley faces and lace."

Ann looked at Spenser. "She told you about that?"

Spenser gushed, "That sounded *so cool.* I wish I'd been there."

"Madison needs practice," said Ann. "We'll take you with us the next time we go."

"Next time?" said Madison, her eyebrows arching upward. "You want me to go shooting again?"

"Absolutely," said Ann. "You shouldn't ignore your poor performance."

"I'll go when you get set up with a date."

"Not negotiable," said Ann.

"The manager of this spa is cute," said Spenser.

Madison whipped her head toward Spenser, her dark silky hair slipping all the way out on one side. "What, Frank?" She slapped her magazine down. "No way!"

"He is, too."

"Not for my mother, he's not!"

"Late thirties, early forties," Spenser continued.

"No way in hell! I'll fight you."

Nika said, "I could arrange a meeting…"

"No!" said Ann and Madison in unison. They looked surprised at one another, having never agreed on the same thing with such passion before.

"Your Russian blood is showing," said Nika, laughing as she stood. "So stubborn. Ann didn't need to do that DNA test," she said with satisfaction. "Now hurry." She picked up her wine glass and headed for the door. "We all have appointments at nail salon."

Ann stood there in shock as Nika walked away. "How did she know I snuck a DNA sample?"

"Seriously?" asked Madison. "With how strong the family resemblance is, you still did a DNA test?"

"Had to make sure," she murmured, watching Nika go. "She's good," she said as she followed her out the door.

Grateful that the gun range issue was temporarily off the table, Madison stood up with Spenser, eager to get her manicure and pedicure.

"You were messing with my head," said Madison, walking behind Spenser, "weren't you?"

"Mostly," said Spenser, trying to not laugh and failing. "But he is cute."

As Spenser left ahead of her, Madison paused inside the waxing salon doorway to rewrap her loose hair towel. With all her hair neatly back in place, she passed through the door. Lettie and another staff member stood nearby in the hallway.

Lettie was in the middle of a sentence "… and Frank's not happy she's here."

Madison hurried away on silent, bare feet.

Chapter Four

As Madison caught up to the others, she heard Nika asking, "Is it true that young women dance with each other in these nightclubs? They don't wait for man to ask them to dance?"

"That's true," said Spenser.

"In my day it was torture," said Nika, "waiting and hoping someone would ask."

Madison couldn't believe Nika ever had to wait for any man. "You went to dances in Russia?"

"Yes, I love to dance."

Madison and Spenser exchanged a knowing smile.

"Do you love to dance, Ann?" asked Nika.

There was a pause as they walked down the hallway. Ann finally answered, "I don't know how to dance. I would just embarrass myself."

Nika seemed taken aback. "You do not dance?"

"No," When there was no response Ann blinked and said, "Why are you so surprised?"

"There have been many discoveries of how much we are alike," said Nika. "Getting to know you these last few weeks has been dream come true, but I never imagined that there would be so many things we have in common." She pulled a strand of hair away from her light green eyes, the eyes almost identical to Madison's that had shocked Madison when she first saw them. Nika continued, "We are both patriots, we have served our countries, we both gave birth to daughters when we were mere teenagers. And Madison tells me you excelled in school, graduating with honors."

"Yes, I did," said Ann.

"So did I," said Nika.

"I was top of the class."

"I was top in our region."

"I was top of several regions."

"And I spent high school in detention," said Madison. "Look, can we not have this competition right now?"

"I don't know what you're talking about," said Ann.

"Nor I," said Nika.

Arriving at the nail salon, they found Brittany just inside the entrance behind a tall counter. She was the hostess. She didn't in any way acknowledge that she'd met Madison earlier, her smile seeming to pass right through her, and Madison figured it was probably for the best.

"Come right in. I'm Brittany." She tossed her long honey brown hair behind her shoulder and flashed them a pleasant smile. "Do you ladies have appointments?"

"Yes," said Nika. "I put all four appointments under my name. Veronica Fedora."

Brittany eyed Nika and blinked. "Oh, so, you're her. I saw the name in the appointments list. You have a VIP account now, right?"

"You know of me?" asked Nika.

"Sure, everyone does. Well, maybe not everyone, I guess. But word gets around." She checked them in on her computer then walked away, calling over her shoulder. "Follow me."

Brittany led them to a wall where hundreds of bottles of nail enamel in a wide range of colors sat in rows, waiting to be chosen. Nika chose an iridescent cinnamon for her manicure, and a brighter blue-red for her pedicure. Spenser picked a dark plum for toes, and a lighter plum for her fingers. Madison wanted cherry-black for her fingers, and a velvety fuchsia for toes. Ann grabbed one bottle of beige pink.

Madison surveyed her mother's complexion and said, "Mom? Would you be willing to try this?" She handed her mother a different color. It was still in the pink family but of a much rosier hue.

"It's kind of dark." Her mother looked doubtful. Madison continued to hold it out to her. Ann stared at it, and then took it. "I'll use it for the pedicure."

Sitting on the waiting couches, Madison asked, "Has anyone decided where they want to go for dinner tonight?"

"How about your place?" said Spenser. "I could use some of your killer pancakes."

"Pancakes for dinner?" said Madison.

"Killer pancakes?" said Nika. "I have not heard these words together."

"She's saying they're delicious," Ann explained.

"Delicious," repeated Nika. "And this could kill you?"

"What kind are they?" Ann asked Madison.

Sheepish, Madison looked at the floor before answering. "Pineapple. I press pineapple rings into the center of the batter before it has a chance to cook." She looked up at her mother, wondering if she would remember.

Ann did. Her eyes grew moist as she said, "You couldn't have been more than, what… four years old that day?"

"Which means you must have been nineteen. Just before you left for college," said Madison, her expression growing shy.

"Oh, Madness," said Ann. "How I regret all those lost years."

Madison smiled at her mother's use of her old pet name for her.

Ann turned to Nika. "The day I left for college, she wanted a can of pineapple for breakfast. I didn't want our last day to have strife, so I put it in the pancakes."

Nika turned to Madison. "And you have been making them ever since?"

"When I get in the mood for them, yes."

"I'm in the mood," said Spenser.

"Me, too," said Ann.

"I should love to have these pancakes," said Nika. "A nice way to die."

"How about it, Madison?" said Spenser with a devious smile "Kill us with pancakes?"

"Spenser, you're more calculating than I give you credit for," said Madison.

"Hey, everyone is good at something."

"I have learned that Madison is good at singing," said Nika, looking proud. "I heard her deliver one of those singing telegrams. She amazes. I cannot sing at all."

Ann said, "I can sing."

Incredulous, Madison and Nika both said, "You can?"

"Well don't be so surprised," said Ann, indignant. "Yes. It just so happens I can sing." She sighed and added, "I just can't dance."

"Perhaps Madison can show us latest dances sometime," said Nika.

"Would you like to see one of those nightclubs?" offered Madison.

"Yes! Yes, I would love to watch dancing. Ann, let's go see it with her and Spenser."

Worried, Ann said, "No one will try to force me to dance, will they?"

Madison shuddered at the thought. No one could force her mother to do anything she didn't want to, that was for damn sure. But she hid a smile, thinking she'd like to see someone try.

"No one will force you to dance," she said. "There won't even be a contest." She gave her mother a knowing smile.

"There was no contest," huffed Ann. "We were just shooting the way we normally would."

"I saw no contest," said Nika.

Yet they both knew I was talking about the gun range. "Sorry. My mistake," said Madison.

Brittany stepped up, her tone cool and professional. "Your manicure tables are ready. We've seated you all next to each other."

As they walked to the four little tables, Brittany stepped directly in front of Madison, face to face, causing Madison to come to an abrupt halt. "Hey, can I have a moment?" Brittany said quietly.

Madison braced herself. "What is it?"

"I wanted to say I'm sorry."

It was a pleasant surprise, yet uncomfortable in its delivery. "No harm done." Madison shrugged. "It's all right."

"It's just that… well, I get what you were trying to do earlier, and the more I thought about it, the more I liked you. I'm not used to people being nice to me."

Madison didn't know what to say as she looked into Brittany's pretty brown eyes. "I'm… so sorry to hear that," she said. Over Brittany's shoulder, Madison saw her mother beckoning to her.

"Madison?" Ann's voice rose in curiosity.

Madison turned her gaze back to Brittany. With sincerity, she said, "There are lots of good people in the world. I hope you get more of them in your life."

Crossing the room to catch up with the other three, Madison took her place at a small table in between her mother and Spenser. The small jar of mud in her pocket bumped the table as she scooted in, the pleasant memory of the massage returning.

Small talk turned to occasional laughter as their hands were manicured by a competent staff. Madison observed their camaraderie and courtesy toward one another, and it seemed that everyone here enjoyed their jobs. She looked at Brittany a few times, standing alone at the station by the door, doing paperwork. Madison felt bad for her, surprised at the notion that people here weren't nice to her. The rest of the staff seemed to get along. It didn't make sense. Unless there was more to the story.

All manicured and dried, the small group returned to the waiting area just as Brittany came and announced, "Three pedicure chairs are available, but it'll be at least ten minutes until the fourth is open."

Looking at Madison, Nika said, "You have time to get something from the wine bar.

"I'm fine," said Madison, leaning back into the couch.

Nika added, "I've noticed there is handsome new man working wine bar. Wine tastes better when handsome man has poured it."

Brittany brushed off the front of her black uniform jacket, mumbling, "He's handsome, but he knows it."

Ignoring Brittany, Nika said, "Perhaps you would like to meet him."

"Uh… actually," Brittany began, "he's my boyfriend. Sorry." She smiled as if the matter were settled. "He's taken."

"Not a problem," said Madison. "I'm seeing someone myself right now." She shook a playful finger at Nika. "You're trying to stir up trouble."

Nika, her face cool and hard, stared at Brittany for a moment. Then she returned her attention to Madison. "I just thought you might be interested. He looked to be your type."

Brittany's smile stayed hard on her face. Through her teeth she said, "But he isn't."

"No, he isn't," said Madison, looking from Brittany to Nika. She knit her brows as she looked at Nika, trying to signal her to stop it.

Nika laughed. "I am sorry. I am doing poor job of hinting that I would like another glass of wine. Would you be so kind, Madison, and bring Ann and myself more wine? Get some for you and Spenser too."

"Of course. Why didn't you say so?" She stood.

Brittany's teeth were still tight as she smiled with an extra dose of sunshine, and cocked her head to the side. "Hurry back," she said in a sing-song tone.

Uncomfortable, Madison decided that getting out of the nail salon for a few minutes would suit her just fine right now. She couldn't put her finger on it and decided she just didn't understand Brittany yet. Perhaps she would, if given more time. The problem was, more time around Brittany was the last thing she wanted.

Stepping into the hallway, Madison decided to take a detour and head back to the dressing room.

At her open locker, she pulled her cell phone from her purse and made a quick call to Phil. "Phil, would I sound paranoid if I asked you whether Iris Alexander is angry with me, or in some way is trying to keep tabs on me?"

"The answer," he replied, "is yes. Yes, you sound paranoid. What the hell are you talking about, Minty?

"I'm at The Lazy Petal and I keep hearing people say something about keeping an eye on me, or calling me a trouble maker. You remember that actor Frank Bergman that I accidentally buried alive?"

Phil erupted into laughter.

"Phil?"

His laughter only increased.

"Phil! How can you still be laughing about that two years later?"

"Sorry, Minty." He slowly gained control of himself. "That is still *the* funniest film shoot mishap I ever heard of. People still ask me to recite that story."

"It wasn't funny!"

"Maybe not to you with Frank trying to chase you down on the set and all. Man, I wish I'd been there to see when the crew tackled him. Did they all sit on him, or was it just one guy?"

Madison closed her eyes and sighed. "It was two guys. They took turns until he came to his senses."

"Ha! Great stuff. Good thing that wasn't a union film. What a mess. But why are you bringing that up? And what does that have to do with Iris?"

"I don't know. That's what's driving me nuts. I told you I'm here at The Lazy Petal? Well Frank is the manager. He wants me followed and I overheard Iris call me a trouble maker and ask where I was."

"You're kidding me. I thought everything was okay with him now. That idiot needs to take stock if he's blaming you for his problems. We all got problems, you know? But Iris? That don't make sense. She likes you."

"How do you figure? I almost ruined her photo shoot. It must be expensive to rent out that Ferris wheel like she did."

"For one thing, Iris could rent that Ferris wheel with her spare change. But the main reason I say that is because she asked for you by name when she called to book the shoot."

"What? Why? How did she even know about me?"

"I never had a chance to ask her. Jen stopped in here to have one of her little tantrums, throwing things at me again. I had to book the shoot as fast as I could and get off the phone."

"I can't believe you put up with that."

"You have to understand. Strippers are high strung, like thoroughbreds and prima ballerinas. They need patience and love."

"She's there right now, listening, isn't she?"

"Yup!"

Hurrying to the wine bar, Madison tried to rehearse what she would say to Frank if she ran into him. It wasn't her fault the coffin refused to open on cue. He was convinced she must've heard him screaming but refused to stop. Madison would never do that to someone, but he was so freaked out that day he wouldn't listen. Would he listen now?

In a low budget indie vampire film, her character's job was to fill the open grave, shoveling the loose dirt onto a coffin as fast as she could. She didn't know the director had set up a surprise for her, hoping to catch her authentic shock when the coffin violently sprang open. But the release button and the springs malfunctioned. No springing coffin lid, no flying dirt. Then the director let her continue to bury the coffin, assuming Frank must be waiting to make it extra dramatic before hitting the release button. No one knew he was having a meltdown in there.

She sighed, remembering that day. Frank had always been a great guy before that. She'd heard he left acting. But obviously he'd found a great position as manager of The Lazy Petal.

As she hurried down the hallway, she came upon the entrance to the pools, the sliding door wide open. Framing the entryway, sheer curtain swags hung in lavish folds and parted like an entrance to an oasis, secret and inviting.

Standing in the entryway, Madison mouthed a silent "wow." On the left side of the spacious room, lush ferns, moss, and rocks formed a tower from which a waterfall poured, splashing delicately into the largest pool. On the right side of the room were three smaller pools for sitting and soaking. A discreet sign by each pool stated the temperature. Pillar candles seemed to be everywhere, with each pillar candle surrounded by tea lights in clear glass candleholders. A gorgeous trestle table, restoration chic, lined the wall nearest the smaller pools. With it's sturdy legs and long table top, it was covered with fresh flowers, folded towels, and more robes.

In dim lighting, nude women climbed in and out of blue pools, while clusters of women in Jacuzzis chatted. Everyone appeared relaxed. The same harp music she'd heard when she first entered the spa accompanied the occasional light splash whenever a woman rose from the water, ascending the stairs. Not a perfect figure in the bunch—real women were taking a break from their lives. It was restful to see.

Remembering the wine, she left the doorway to the pools and continued down the hallway. It was important that Ann and Nika find a way to develop a real connection with each other or, at the very least, be allowed to try. It was clear that they wanted to, but they were both trying so hard to impress that they were bragging about their accomplishments. Maybe more wine would help those two.

Straight ahead at the end of the hallway was a black curtain marked with a Staff Only sign, but to the right a set of doors led into the wine bar lounge. Passing through the doors, she entered a co-ed area of the spa.

With upholstered couches and chairs, and a curved marble counter complete with wine bottles of various labels, the lounge looked inviting. Across the room a second door said Staff Only. It was closed. Not one patron was in the whole place. Hopefully Brittany's boyfriend would be quick.

As she approached the bar, she slowed down and stared in confusion. Behind the counter was a tall, lean, and muscular guy with curly brown hair and full lips. As he wiped down the counter, his biceps filled out the sleeves of the spa's black uniform shirt. It was Jason Clark, the guy she had recently been dating.

Chapter Five

Picking up empty wine bottles, he vanished through black curtains that hid a small room behind the bar. As Madison approached, he returned with a rack of clean wine glasses, setting it on the counter. Raising his head, his eyes zeroed in on her with mild surprise and enthusiasm. She could see he was taking in the view of her in a plush robe with a towel on her head. His smile was knowing, his hazel brown eyes come-hither, making Madison melt at the sight of him.

She wanted to slap herself. *Hang on to yourself, girl. You need to find out what the hell is going on!*

"Well," he said. "Glad I stuck around a few more hours. Today is my last day." He set new bottles of wine on the counter. She heard his cell phone's ring tone, and he pulled it out of his hip pocket, his eyes creasing as he stared at the screen. "And that is why," he said quietly. He hit a button, stopping the ring tone, and set the phone aside on the counter, his smile gone.

"What's the matter?" she asked.

"Long story." He looked at her, his smile returning, and said, "But the important thing is, what can I do for you?" He leaned across the counter. "And yes, that was a loaded question." He wagged his eyebrows in playful drama.

Ignoring the urge to flirt back, she said, "I didn't know you worked here."

"Temporary. The last guy fell or something, they're not sure. I used to work here last year, so they asked me to fill in until they find someone else."

"Well, I was just talking to an interesting person. You never know who you might run into in this place."

"I'll bet I know," he said. "Don't worry. I didn't take her too seriously."

"Well, she thinks you did."

"No way. She had me going for a minute there, but what really caught my attention were her gorgeous eyes. I told her so and that's how we met."

"Oh, really." Annoyed, she remembered that first day when he told her how beautiful her eyes were. "Is that the line you use on girls?"

"Line?" He laughed. "She started it. I couldn't believe she was actually flirting with me. Then I recognized her eyes. You didn't tell me your grandmother was a cougar."

"What?" asked Madison, surprised. "You mean Nika? I didn't know. That she's a cougar, I mean. She is? Are you sure?"

"Nah, she was just giving me a hard time," he chuckled. "But she could be a cougar if she wanted to. No one would believe she's your grandmother."

Partly relieved, she laughed. "No, I know. It's crazy, isn't it?"

"She told me she was going to send you to the wine counter. Aren't I supposed to be pouring you some wine or something?"

"Yeah. But there's someone else I have to ask about."

His phone went off again. He stared at it on the counter and rubbed his forehead. "I have to take this or she won't stop calling."

He picked up the phone, took a deep breath and hit the button. His face turned hard and a forced polite tone took over. "Hello, Brittany." He worked his jaw as he listened. "I'm fine. And you?" He listened. "No, you're not bugging me," he said as he rolled his eyes. "It's nice to hear you too, but look, you shouldn't be calling me and... what?" His face froze. His eyes grew wide. "Uh... yeah... there's a girl here." There was fear on his face. "I don't know. Hold on." He held the phone away from his face and said, unnaturally loud, "Excuse me, miss. Is your name Madison?"

She didn't know if she was more surprised by his question, or by the robot way in which he'd said it. "What—"

As fast as lightning, he put his hand over her mouth, pleading with his eyes. There was a desperate quality to his nonchalant reply. "Why, yes," he said into the phone, "Her name *is* Madison."

Into his hand Madison said, "What the hell are you doing?" But her muffled words came out sounding like "Utta-eleroo-doon?"

"There's a long line here, Brittany," he said into his phone. "I need to go now. I'll tell her. Okay, bye." He hung up and pulled his hand away from her mouth.

"Tell me what?" she said with some heat.

He stared at the phone in his hand. "This can't be happening," he said, his shoulders slumping. He looked up at Madison. "She says they're ready for you." In a timid voice he added "Uh… do you want some wine?"

"Spill it," she said.

"The wine?"

"Brittany."

"Brittany?" he squeaked.

"Is that panic I see in your eyes?"

"More like blind terror," he said. "If she finds out I'm seeing you, my life will revert to hell."

"And pray tell, *why* is that? And this better be good."

He looked around the empty lounge, and then leaned in with a quiet voice. "Because she is the psycho ex-girlfriend that legends are made from. Guys tell Brittany-stories around the campfire to scare the shit out of each other. If she had theme music it would be screaming staccato violin strings."

Madison blinked. "Okay." She swallowed. "That was pretty good."

Jason's eyes darted toward the doors and back to Madison. "Spotted her this morning. That's why I quit. If I'd known she worked here…"

"Were you together a long time?"

"A week. In that time she acted like we were surgically attached. I got more creeped out each day," said Jason. "She'll do anything for attention."

"Why didn't you tell me about her?"

"It was a year ago!" He dropped his arms in frustration. "Besides, you haven't told me about all your boyfriends yet. Am I in for some surprises?"

"What do you mean?"

"Am I going wake up to find someone has scratched my full name into my boss's car?"

"No."

"Burned it into my neighbor's lawn?"

"No."

"Shaved it on my dog's butt?"

"No!"

"Just checking."

"That's crazy!"

"That's Brittany."

"She did that?"

"On a good day."

Madison's mouth fell open.

"She finally got it out of her system and left me alone. I want to keep it that way, so please don't tell her you know me." He pulled out a bottle of red wine, uncorked it, and set glasses on the counter.

"But…"

"Nika's drinking pinot noir, right?"

"Sure, whatever," said Madison, trying to wrench her attention back to the wine.

"We have to hurry," he said. "She must suspect something or she wouldn't have called. Three glasses?"

"Four. But… this is crazy."

He pulled up a tray, setting the wine glasses on it. "I'm just heading off trouble. I can't afford to wake the sleeping psycho." His hand started to shake as he poured. "I just want to get through this day, then I'll be gone. I've moved since last year and she doesn't know where… what am I saying?" With his head hanging, he set the bottle down, his hand still wrapped around its neck. "Of course she'll know. I'll probably find her in my house again tonight."

"She broke into your house before?"

"Or teleported. I never heard a thing. I just rolled over in bed and bumped into her."

"What?"

"Scared the shit out of me." He corked the bottle. "Maybe I should just go now."

"That was a year ago?"

"Yeah, but it feels like yesterday."

"But when she called, she was asking about me, right?"

"Well, yeah…"

"I really do have an appointment for a pedicure right now. That's why she called. In fact, I'll bet it was hard for her to call you. She might be embarrassed about the past."

"Brittany? Embarrassed? Ha!"

Madison sighed. She put her elbows on the counter and rubbed her face with her hands. "I don't know, Jason. This feels weird."

"I just want to end this day peacefully and go home. Please, I'm begging you."

Madison turned her palms to the air in a surrendering gesture. "Okay, okay fine. I'll go along with it. I won't tell Brittany a thing. You stay peaceful, Brittany stays peaceful, we'll have peaceful pedicures, and everyone goes home happy."

He expelled a long breath, which ended with, "Thank you." He grabbed her face between his hands in a sudden kiss, expressing relief and gratitude at first. But heat soon replaced the gratitude as his lips sought to dominate her mouth, his tongue exploring. He ended the kiss with a gentle suction on her lower lip.

When he pulled away, Madison was still leaning forward over the counter, lost in a kiss no longer happening. What was it he was thanking her for? She wanted to be thanked some more. Then it hit her that her lips were still parted and her eyes were still closed. Self-conscious, she straightened up and looked around, hoping no one saw that.

"Sorry," he said. "That wasn't appropriate for this place. I won't do it again."

"Oh, uh, no problem. I didn't mind. Not judging." She shook her head. "Not bothered at all. Well, I mean not bothered in *that* way, maybe in other ways…"

"I'll make it up to you, I swear," he said, picking up the wine tray and setting it down in front of her.

"Make what up?" said Madison.

"Making you pretend you don't know me."

"Oh that! Yeah, like you said, all you have to do is get through this day. Then you'll be gone, no more drama, you can relax…"

From across the room a sweet sing-song voice cut in. "Madison. There you are."

They jumped and Madison spun around to face Brittany, who walked up with a pleasant smile.

Brittany said, "I'm sorry, I didn't mean to startle you. Our calendar is full today so we need to get you back to the salon." She looked around the empty lounge area. "I see the long line has subsided." She looked Jason directly in the eyes, her smile turning coy.

A trickle of sweat rolled down the side of his face.

"Hello Jason," she said.

With a closed-lipped half-smile, Jason gave one firm nod in her direction then looked down, busying himself with taking the clean wine glasses out of the rack.

She continued, "Aren't you going to say hello?" She tilted her head, her eyes half lidded. "I saw the way you were looking at me this morning." With a sexy smile, her voice breathy, she said, "You bad boy."

"Brittany," he said, "please don't. I have work to do."

Surprise in her eyes, she stared at Jason. Impatiently she said, "Lighten up. I was just playing with you." She straightened the lapels of her black jacket as her mouth took on a firm line, her chin tilting up. "You don't know this, but I'm about to get a big promotion. I'll have influence and I could get you a raise."

"Even if Frank offered me a raise—" Jason began.

"Forget Frank," she said. "He doesn't matter. Just wait one more day before you quit. You'll see."

"I'm leaving at the end of my shift," he said, trying for a friendly tone. "I hope you have a nice life."

"But…"

"Let it go," he said, more firmly.

Sighing, she said, "Not a problem." She turned to Madison and said, "Let me get this for you." She picked up the tray with the wine glasses on it, but before turning to go, she said, "Jason? Would it be all right if you turned up the music?"

"I don't think so," he said. "It might be against policy." Madison saw the volume controls located at the side of the counter, about waist level. Jason moved to stand in front of them, his face firm.

Brittany's hopeful smile couldn't quite reach her sad eyes. "I'm sorry. I didn't mean anything by it. I just think the music is pretty."

Watching her, Madison tried to imagine the crazy behavior that Jason described, but it was hard to picture. She found herself wondering if he was perhaps... not *lying* exactly... but exaggerating for effect. Maybe he was remembering how it felt, instead of how it actually was. He looked at Madison and they locked eyes for a second before he quickly looked away.

"It's all right if you look at Madison," said Brittany, resigned.

"I wasn't looking at her," Jason lied.

"It's all right. She has a boyfriend." Her voice was gentle and her expression a bit sad. "You need to try to act like a normal person, Jason."

"That's rich," he mumbled.

Jason wiped spilled drops of wine from the counter. Brittany stood in the same place for a few moments watching Jason as he kept wiping a counter that was already clean. Madison fidgeted, looking around for something she could pretend to get engrossed in. She wished she were somewhere else so Brittany and Jason could work out their bygones. The more Jason clung to his stoic silence, the more she felt sorry for Brittany.

Madison took the tray from her. "I know the way back. I'll see you there." Jason shot her a desperate look that gave her pause.

"I'm sorry," said Brittany. "I shouldn't have delayed you." She inhaled and expelled her breath quickly as if giving up. "We both need to get back." She straightened her shoulders and tossed her honey brown hair behind her shoulder, smiling.

Madison tried to smile back. "Okay."

They turned together and left the wine bar, Brittany holding the door open for Madison who was now carrying the tray. Madison was torn between wanting to help Brittany, and wanting to run from her. It was becoming obvious that Brittany had a way of burning bridges. *If you burn bridges, people will follow their instincts and steer clear.*

As they re-entered the Women Only area, Brittany said, "He doesn't know it, but he owes me his job. I knew he used to work here, so when Barry had an accident, I suggested they bring Jason back."

"Was Barry the last wine server?"

"Yeah."

"What exactly happened to Barry?"

"He hurt his little head." She changed the subject. "I'm sorry you had to witness that back there. I guess you could tell that we're not exactly together right now."

"Oh. It's none of my business," said Madison.

"We had some problems and had to split up. He was upset of course, but he needed to get his act together." She sighed, adding, "And I needed the space."

Madison kept walking, keeping her face placid. Was there such a thing as break-up therapy, where the couple straightens out who broke up with whom? Hearing Brittany's version made her feel antsy, and she wished she could tell Brittany the truth and make a clean break from the deception.

But I have to help end the day peacefully.

Brittany continued, "It's important that I believe what's going to be true, and not what used to be true."

"Absolutely. It's important to believe… wait, what?"

"I have to focus on what's going to be true," explained Brittany. "He's going to get his act together, I just know it. Then our timeout can be over."

The wine glasses on Madison's tray jostled a bit. "Timeout? I thought you said you broke up."

"No, I said we had to split up," said Brittany. "That's not the same as breaking up."

"It's not?"

"No, of course not," said Brittany with a chuckle. "What a crazy idea."

Madison's face froze for a moment as they continued walking. Shifting the tray to one hand, she picked up a glass with the other, taking a few big swallows.

Brittany's smile grew. "Once our timeout is over, I'll make him glad he waited for me." Her eyes sparkled. "I'll ride him so hard he'll beg me to never leave him again."

Madison wanted to shove her hair towel down over her ears, or maybe into Brittany's mouth. "Gosh, that's… private," said Madison. "It's not something I should…"

"You can tell he wants me," said Brittany.

"… no."

"He'll love me with all the fierce passion he has in his body."

"Oh… boy."

Chapter Six

"Gosh, I'm holding everyone up at the nail salon," said Madison. "I should hurry." She picked up the pace, Brittany staying in step with her.

"What about you and your boyfriend?" asked Brittany. "Have you ever taken a timeout?"

"Actually, he's not my boyfriend yet, I mean we just started dating."

"I don't understand."

"You know, that period of time when you're still getting to know each other? You're trying to decide if someone is right for you."

Brittany stared. "I don't get it."

"Dating is like reading the recipe before you start cooking. You want to understand what it is you're getting into."

"Wow. You like it complicated."

"Well…" Madison came up with an idea. "It's because guys can drive you crazy," she said, pleased with herself that she'd come up with this universal line to say. "Can't figure them out."

Brittany nodded. "Yeah," she said. "They never listen or pay attention when you have something important to say."

"Oh, I know. You have to practically wave your arms, 'Hello!'"

Brittany smirked. "Then they turn their head in your direction but their eyes are still on the game."

"Some days you'd have to be bleeding," said Madison, "just to get their attention."

"You're right!"

They laughed together as they passed the waxing salon. Madison added, "Thank goodness not all guys are like that. Most guys are all right."

"What planet are you from?" asked Brittany. "Because there's not one man on planet Earth who isn't a pig."

Madison sputtered, searching for some footing in the presence of a man-hater. This became more difficult by the moment. She scrambled for a way to salvage the safe place she'd finally found with Brittany. "Um… I like bacon?"

Brittany giggled, and then sighed. "It's so nice to meet someone who understands."

Madison's smile was crooked. She felt like a rat. But damn, Brittany made her nervous. The last thing she wanted was to get on her bad side.

"Is Veronica your grandmother?" asked Brittany.

"Yes."

Brittany nodded like she understood. "It's hard to live up to your family's expectations. You and I have a lot in common. We should get together, don't you think?"

Madison choked. She had no clue what Brittany meant about having anything in common. "I uh, don't actually live around here," she lied. "I'm visiting my mom."

"Well, look me up when you come into town," said Brittany, smiling.

Madison nodded as she withered inside, knowing she'd have to climb down from a mountain of guilt when this was over.

We just have to get through this day.

As they passed the pool entryway, Madison knew she shouldn't ask, but she couldn't resist. "So why did you guys take some time apart?"

"He was too clingy and expected me to do everything with him. I never had any time to myself without him accusing me of cheating." She shrugged her shoulders in a matter-of-fact way. "It's not healthy to be with someone who's so needy."

Madison worked to control her face. *That explains everything... in Opposite Land.* She tried a nonchalant tone. "I guess it's best to face reality."

"Oh, I'm all about reality," said Brittany. "Sometimes a person has to move on. So if I find out he has any more excuses, I'll end it. Permanently."

They entered the nail salon and found Ann, Nika, and Spenser sitting high in elevated leather chairs. Their feet soaked in small copper tubs of water in which rose petals swirled, making a merry chase of floating lemon slices. Each woman had a manicurist sitting on a short stool by her tub, working on a foot while the other foot continued to soak.

Ann and Nika held a lively conversation, hardly noticing Madison as she set their glasses of wine on the little side tables next to them. Spenser looked at Madison with sympathy in her eyes, tilting her head toward the other two. Madison took the cue and braced herself.

Brittany returned to her station by the front door while Madison made her way to the empty chair between Ann and Nika. She sat, putting her feet into the copper tub of water the manicurist had prepared for her. It felt warm and wonderful. The rose petals and lemon slices dived down with her feet, then sprang back up in a watery bounce. Her manicurist took a seat on the stool.

"And maybe," said Ann, "if they had allowed their citizens more freedom to travel away from the Soviet

Union, they would have learned more hospitable manners."

Madison looked to her right at her mother. "You're not carrying on the Cold War again, are you?" But her question fell on deaf ears.

"Hospitable?" said Nika, causing Madison to look to her left. "There was time when Americans were not so accepting of us. Back then, I would not have called them hospitable. I could tell you stories."

"I don't need to be told stories," said Ann. "I have plenty of my own, thank you, and I would never…"

Madison cut in with a loud voice, "Walnuts or pecans? Which is best? Discuss."

Silently, they focused their gazes on her. She was caught in a stare-down sandwich. Unsure which direction to look, she drank her wine and faced straight ahead, her eyes furtively glancing side to side as she waited to see if she'd get away with her rudeness.

Ann mumbled, "I don't like nuts."

"Neither do I," said Nika. Madison wondered if she should've left them alone, when Nika added "Well… except for pistachios."

Ann looked around Madison at Nika. "You like pistachios?"

In a passionate voice, Nika said, "I love them."

Ann's eyes grew wide. "So do I."

"Have you tried chocolate covered pistachios?" asked Nika, getting excited.

"Yes! I *love* those! But I can never find them."

"I know what you mean," said Nika. "And when I do run into them, I—"

"Buy them all?"

"Yes," Nika laughed.

"Me too."

"They always look at me like I'm crazy," said Nika.

Ann took a moment, observing Nika with fascination. "There's a new store I've been meaning to try. If they have them, I'll get them for you."

In a soft voice, Nika said, "Thank you."

A silence followed as they all leaned back into their chairs and drank their wine. Madison looked past Ann to Spenser sitting in the next chair. She reached her glass across her mother to clink with Spenser. "Score one for the home team."

Ann wore a resigned half-smile. "We get your point. You don't have to gloat."

Nika turned her attention to Madison and said, "And thank *you*."

"For what?" said Madison.

Nika smiled and shrugged. "For being most beautiful granddaughter any woman could want."

With a wry look, Ann said, "It doesn't hurt that she inherited a bit of that from you, does it?"

With a smug pout, Nika said, "No, it does not. And she has your lovely skin and beautiful smile. Your proud nose, too."

"Okay, you can stop now," said Madison. Her manicurist dried each foot and stuffed cotton balls between each toe.

But Nika leaned forward, looking past Madison to Ann. With a conspiratorial tone, she said, "She also has fierce look when she is angry or indignant."

"Oh, you've caught that?" said Ann.

"Have I mentioned the weather?" said Madison. "Looks like rain."

Nika continued with Ann. "How could I not? You should have seen her last month when I first met her and all that trouble was breaking loose."

"Although, it *is* Seattle after all," said Madison.

"You probably wondered," said Ann, "how on earth you were going to control her."

"Peter Piper picked a peck of pickled peppers."

"You can't control her," said Nika, shaking her head. "I found this out."

"Don't I know it," said Ann, resigned.

"Don't mind me. I'll just be sitting here in the middle," said Madison, "you know, in case you have any questions or want to check my teeth." All the flattery and commentary on her behavior made her a tad self-conscious, but she had to admit their conversation was an improvement over the old Cold War arguments.

Her manicurist finished one foot and began working on the other, painting each toe with the velvety fuchsia. Madison thought the color was splendid. She relaxed in the chair, enjoying the sight of all four women getting pretty toes. She felt silly about placing such a high value on this experience, but it seemed to her that there was a chumminess developing. After so many years of her mother's absence, she was finally getting to know her in the common everyday way. And although things were a bit complicated with Veronica "Nika" Fedora coming into their lives, Madison knew she had a rare opportunity to help her mother get to know *her* own mother.

Ann and Nika seemed to be getting along in their weird argumentative way. Things were looking up. *Maybe they simply like to debate. Maybe I'm taking it too hard when they don't agree.* She had to admit, they were a lot alike when it came to being opinionated.

As Madison took a sip of her wine, Nika smiled and asked, "Well? Did you see your handsome Jason? Were you surprised?"

Brittany looked up from her station at the front counter by the door.

"Uh…" Madison uttered.

Ann joined in. "Nika said you've been dating him. It's Jason Clark, isn't it? The one I already met?"

Brittany locked eyes with Madison, her gaze fixed, her face not moving a fraction. Madison could swear Brittany's eyes… emptied.

"Curly brown hair. Hazel brown eyes," Madison heard Nika saying.

"That's the one," said Ann. "He's a good boy. Good family."

Brittany's stare was cold and deliberate as her face took on a quality that made Madison feel weighed and assessed. Trying to retain a casual expression, Madison raised her wine glass for a sip.

Brittany's hands reached down into a desk drawer.

Madison's wine glass came to a dead stop at her lips, her body going on alert.

But Brittany merely pulled out a nail file, held up the middle finger on her left hand and began to file that nail.

"I haven't met him yet," said Spenser, "but he sounds dreamy."

"I told him he was handsome and he blushed." Nika sipped her wine.

Ann smiled. "You're kidding me."

The middle fingernail that Brittany held up was getting pointier and sharper.

"Can you believe it?" Nika continued. "Man who blushes at compliment is hard to find. Of course, now he may think I am leopard."

"A what?" Ann tucked a strand of dark hair back under the edge of her towel.

"Leopard. Woman who chases young men."

Ann corrected her. "You mean a cougar. The word they use is cougar."

"Cougar? But leopard is sexier."

Madison blinked, pulling her eyes away from Brittany and smiling at her mother. She hoped they wouldn't notice Brittany's behavior or her own worry, but Spenser caught her eye and gave a subtle upward nod in Brittany's direction, a question in her eyes. Madison shook her head, a signal to Spenser that she couldn't talk about it right now.

Ann chuckled with her face in her hand. "A leopard," she said. "I love it."

"I thought that was how you say it," said Nika, trying not to laugh.

Madison looked back at Brittany. She was on the phone, calm and cool, no doubt conducting business for the spa. After ending the call, she sorted through paperwork on the counter, making neat piles.

Nika leaned in to Madison and murmured, "I do not trust that girl. Was she rude in wine bar?"

"No," said Madison quietly. "She flirted with Jason, but he wasn't having it. Then she asked him to turn up the harp music, and he wouldn't even do that. I felt sorry for her at the time, but now, frankly, she makes me nervous. I'm not sure what we're dealing with here."

"She knows about you and Jason?"

With a resigned smirk, Madison said, "She does *now*."

"I could not believe she followed you to wine bar," said Nika.

"She told me she wasn't used to people being nice to her." Madison kept her voice low. "But I think it's because she says things that are unsettling. And Jason… well you should've heard what *he* said about her. Really weird stuff."

"There is fine line between crazy, and willing to act crazy to get what you want. I think sane person can choose. But this one?" Nika shook her head. "Not certain. Crazy or not, she will cause big trouble. You learn to sense these things."

Brittany removed her black uniform jacket, folding it neatly.

"What can you do about it?" asked Madison.

"If she wants rope, you let her hang it."

"What?"

"It is American saying," said Nika quietly. "She may want rope."

"You mean 'give them enough rope and they'll hang themselves'?"

"Yes. That is how to say it."

Ann raised her foot, scrutinizing the rose color on her toenails. "What do you think?"

"It looks right for you," said Nika.

"Ooh, that's pretty," said Spenser.

"I like it more than I thought I would." Ann wiggled a toe.

Spenser lifted her foot too, looking back and forth from Ann's toes to her own. "I wish I'd picked your color."

With their pedicures done, Ann and Nika delicately stepped out of the chairs. The cotton balls stuffed between their toes made each stride short and wobbly. Madison and Spenser followed them.

"Can you imagine dancing," asked Nika, "right after pedicure like this?"

Ann said, "You mean with the cotton still between your toes?"

Nika executed a perfectly awkward combination of steps while her arms made wavy motions in the air. She moved more like a drunken sailor than a dancer.

Ann fought a smile. "That's probably how I look when I dance."

Nika offered her hand to Ann while taking a bow. "May I have this dance?"

"Oh, what the hell," said Ann, taking her hand. They did a ridiculous waltz together, robes, hair towels, cotton balls and all. Madison and Spenser watched in fascinated disbelief.

"Madison," said Spenser quietly, "are they doing this for your benefit?"

"I don't think so." Madison watched them. "They know I want them to get along, of course, but I think it's gone past that now. It's like they're… playing."

"It's not *like* they're playing. They *are* playing."

"Maybe it's the wine?" Nika and Ann began to laugh at themselves as Madison added, "If they got along all the time, I'd probably take it for granted. The fact that they're both so temperamental means you have to enjoy it while it's here."

She couldn't resist stealing a glance at Brittany just one more time, and caught her staring back with an intensity that startled Madison. Brittany held up that middle fingernail she'd been filing to a sharp point and pressed it into her cheek.

What the…?

Slowly, with unrelenting pressure, she dragged it downward, unblinking…

Oh my god!

…as she stared at Madison, slicing a thin red bloody line down the side of her face.

Madison's eyes widened and her heart raced. The sight of such savagery, self-inflicted, held her silent gaze as a single drop of blood collected along Brittany's jawline and fell to the counter. Spellbound, she watched Brittany calmly pick up her purse and walk out the door.

She's freaking mental! Totally running with scissors!

Wrenching her attention away from Brittany's exit, she looked down at the floor, pretending to rub her eyes while she got control. *Let it go! Let it go! Don't let them see it on your face.*

Spenser reached over, putting her hand on Madison's arm. She whispered, "Hey. What's wrong?"

The more she tried to dismiss that picture from her mind, the harder it became to be the only one who saw it. Earlier, she'd hoped no one would see Brittany's behavior, but now she wished she'd pointed it out while it was happening.

"Long story," said Madison.

"Give me the short version."

At a quick pace, Madison said, "I lied for Jason, Nika spilled the beans, Brittany's a bloody psycho, and now she might teleport to his bed."

Spenser raised her brows. "What?"

"Or shave his dog's butt. Either way, it's bad."

Spenser sighed. "Have I mentioned this stuff only happens to you?"

"I have to go warn Jason. I'll try to make it fast."

Spenser studied her for a moment. "All right. But after that, come back and stay with us. Don't let Brittany give you hoops to jump through."

Madison looked over to Nika and Ann, who were deep in a conversation that made them nod and laugh. "It's just that they're having such a nice time. I can't let Brittany ruin it."

"Well, what do I say when they ask about you?" asked Spenser.

"Say what they expect to hear," she said, shrugging. "Say I went to see Jason."

She darted into the hallway, keeping an eye out for Brittany. When she'd left, she had removed her uniform jacket and taken her purse, giving the impression that she was going home. But Madison wasn't buying it. Anyone who gave a parting shot by cutting their own face was either disturbed, or sending a message.

Or both.

Chapter Seven

THE MORE MADISON thought about it, the more she realized Spenser was right.

Waddling down the hallway with cotton balls still stuffed between her toes, she realized she'd been treated to a front row seat to The Brittany Show, featuring psycho ex-girlfriend drama. Mentally disturbed or not, this girl knew how to get attention, and Madison feared she was way out of her league. She'd better tread lightly. Who knew how far Brittany would be willing to go?

Right now all she wanted to do was warn Jason. Tomorrow, she would try to tell Frank about what happened today. If he would listen.

She slipped through the white-curtained entryway into the dimly lit pool room, wishing she were there under different circumstances. The candlelight glowed peacefully, reflected on the water and the wet faces and shoulders of women sitting in the pools, chatting about their lives, their plans, their hopes. High-pitched laughter came from the coldest pool as friends accepting a dare took their first steps into the chilly water.

This peaceful room provided a place for Madison to hide for a brief moment. Listening to the sounds of occasional splashing and the fountain waterfall, she pulled out the little jar of mud from her pocket and spread it all over her face. Hopefully this would buy her more anonymity in the hallway; perhaps give her enough time to get to Jason and have a private conversation. Putting the jar back in her pocket, she used one of the folded towels to wipe the excess mud from her hand.

The volume of the harp music suddenly blasted, causing Madison to jerk and drop the towel. Women in the pools looked up and around at the weirdly loud yet beautiful tones. The slow harp music seemed warped and sick to be so loud and aggressive. It was now louder than any of the ladies' gentle splashing, or even the waterfall that poured into the pool.

Madison knew why the music was so loud.

She ran down the hall, wincing at the cotton between her toes. Up ahead she saw five or six robed women in animated discussion congregating around the doors to the wine bar, their faces scrunched up in annoyance. She knew the best disguise was a crowd, so she joined the herd of towel heads as they marched into the wine bar lounge.

"… a joke of some kind?"

"... rattled my nerves..."

"... not funny..."

Lettie came running in from the staff door on the other side of the lounge. *Oh great!* Madison didn't know if her mud mask was a good enough disguise for an up-close encounter. She tried to keep her eyes lowered enough to hide their green color.

Lettie rushed around them to get behind the counter, searching the area frantically until she found the music controls at the side of the counter. The harp music continued its assault as Lettie squinted at the knobs, trying to read their tiny labels. She finally figured out the proper knob and turned down the volume, but continued to look around the counter and at the curtains, her brows lowered as if trying to make sense of what had just happened. The ladies' excited chatter filled the lounge.

"Where's the wine server?" asked the woman next to Madison.

"I don't know," said Lettie, confused, as she poked her head inside the back curtains.

A man's deep voice barked, "Lettie!" She jumped and spun around as a forty-something man with dark hair and the spa's black uniform shirt entered the lounge from the staff door.

It was Frank Bergman.

"Thank goodness that's over," said one of the women, turning to leave.

"But who did it?" asked a younger woman as she tightened her robe tie.

Frank barked again. "Where is Jason? He said he would finish the shift."

Madison stayed toward the back of the group, peeking between the heads of the women in front.

"I don't know," said Lettie. "He's not here."

Turning to the women nearby, Frank said, "I'm sorry, ladies. Did any of you see anything, maybe someone running away?"

They looked at one another, shrugging, saying "no" or shaking their heads. Like little detectives, they compared notes with one another on where they were and what they were doing when the music blasted.

Frank rubbed his hand down his face. "Well, we apologize for any disturbance. We'll figure it out."

"Thank you ladies," said Lettie. "Please help yourselves to the wine and enjoy your stay with us."

Madison stayed close to the pack, stepping up to the counter with them to pick up a wine glass.

"Where's the pinot noir?" mumbled a lady who wore a mud mask. The sight of her gave Madison confidence that she was blending in.

"That's my favorite, too," said another woman.

"They can blast the music more often if it gets us more wine," said a third lady. They seemed content to joke with one another, quickly forgetting about wanting to know why the music had been so loud in the first place.

Frank closed his eyes, rubbing his temples. "He must be in the break room."

Lettie told Frank quietly, "I think he went home early."

"Well, I wouldn't blame him," he said, his irritation growing. "But humor me and check the break room, after you tell me what the hell is going on."

"I'd say it was a prank," Lettie said.

Madison grabbed a bottle of cabernet sauvignon and slowly poured as she listened.

"I don't mean the music." He brought his voice down, saying, "I told you to keep an eye on Brittany."

"I have." Lettie's tone was cool but assertive. "She's fine and doing an excellent job."

Madison's hand jerked causing the bottle to clink against the glass. *It wasn't me she was supposed to be watching?* She set the bottle on the counter, watching the last drops leave a red trail down its label and form a circle at the bottom of the bottle. The ladies laughed, caught up in their own humor as they clicked their glasses.

"Then why am I getting strange calls about Brittany in the hallway?" murmured Frank.

Trying to get a bit closer to the quiet conversation, Madison stepped over to a trash receptacle at the extreme end of the wine counter. With her back to Frank and

Lettie, she held on to the counter with one hand while she bent over, lifting each foot, removing the cotton balls casually, throwing them one at a time into the trash container as she listened.

Lettie stiffened. "What about her?"

He kept his baritone voice soft, leaning in to say, "They're saying there's blood on her face and red wine all down her clothes. I'm telling you, there's something wrong with that girl."

Madison purposely missed the trash can, throwing a few of the cotton balls on the floor. She then slowly picked them up to stall for time.

Walking back to the staff door, Frank grumbled quietly to Lettie, who followed his every step. "Why is it whenever I try to schedule a dental appointment, all hell breaks loose around here? This tooth is killing me."

"Keep your appointment this time. I insist," said Lettie. "I'll handle everything on this end."

"All right, but don't give her an inch." Frank reached for the doorknob. "I'm sorry, Lettie. I let you give her a chance, but too many weird things happen when she's around. Jason even quit to avoid her."

"We have to be fair, Frank. We should at least question Jason's new girlfriend. Brittany called me from the nail salon, and said the girl threatened her. Called her a psycho."

"And you believed that?"

"You said so yourself, she had blood on her cheek."

That's it! I've had it! Madison stormed toward them, intent on getting a few things straight.

"Her name is Madison Cruz," said Lettie.

"Shit!" said Frank.

Madison whirled around, scurrying back to the counter. The women enjoying their wine in the bar turned their heads toward Frank, their laughter dying away in the wake of his outburst. "Here?" he said. "At The Lazy Petal?"

"Well yes," said Lettie, puzzled.

He exhaled. "This day isn't hard enough. Now I have to face *her*?"

"Aren't you the one who set up her account?"

"No," he said. "Forget the break room. We'll find Jason later. He's here somewhere. But right now get over to the nail salon and get Madison's story. I want her here when I get back. This has been a long time coming."

Taking her wine glass with her as a prop, Madison tried to look casual as she walked toward the spa doors. *If he didn't set up the account... then who?*

She heard the jingle of car keys as he added, "I'll be at the dentist, which sounds pretty damn pleasant right now." He closed the staff door with a firm thump as Madison walked out into the hallway, her pedicured toes back on the marble floor.

She had to think fast. Instead of telling Lettie or Frank that she witnessed Brittany cutting her own face, she decided to talk to Jason first. She hoped the incidents he'd described involving Brittany were documented somehow… maybe with witnesses? Something. Madison's story would be hard to believe without some record of Brittany's past. But how would she get to him? She didn't even know where the break room was.

Why did Brittany have wine on her clothes? She didn't like the sound of that, as if Brittany and Jason were playing tug of war with a glass of wine.

She decided to get her cell phone from her locker to call Jason. No matter where the break room was, he'd most likely have his cell phone on him.

Lettie came barreling past her just then, heading for the nail salon. The mud on Madison's face was getting itchy, but she was glad to still have it on in case Lettie looked back. Then again, Lettie appeared to be in a hurry, weaving in and out of all the robed women with towels on their heads. She may not have been following Madison before, but she sure as hell was after her now. It burned Madison that Brittany had reversed the roles, accusing *her* of being the psycho.

She needed to get to the locker room but she would have to pass the nail salon to get there. If Lettie came out of the nail salon too soon, she would practically bump into Madison.

Up ahead, Lettie was passing the pool entryway.

If I hurry I can get inside the pool area and wait for Lettie to leave the nail salon.

Leaving her wine glass on a nearby table of flowers, she took off at a trot. Hanging onto her head towel, she stepped lively around other women, mumbling apologies for her haste. As she neared the pool entryway, she was also getting closer to Lettie and the nail salon ahead. If Lettie happened to look back, she'd see a towel-headed idiot with mud on her face, running amok. *Just keep walking, Lettie. Don't look back.*

A few more steps and she ducked through the white curtain swags of the pool entryway. She made her way to a table stacked with folded towels. Grabbing one, she returned to the edge of the entryway, standing just within the sheer curtain swags, removing the mud from her face while she watched to see when Lettie would enter the nail salon. Even though she had hung on to her head towel while she ran, the towel was falling off. She pulled it off for a moment to rewrap it, but just as she did, Lettie reached the nail salon door, and sailed right past it.

What? Where is she going in such a hurry if not the nail salon? Confused, Madison kept watching her. Her hair towel hanging limp in her hand, her dark silky hair loose on her shoulders, she slowly leaned further and further out of the entryway, trying to keep her eyes on Lettie as the distance between them grew.

A voice from behind her said, "Hiding from Lettie?"

Chapter Eight

MADISON TURNED AROUND. Clare stood there, smiling and holding a supply bag of tea lights. "I saw her walk by," she said in a secretive tone. "No one would blame you. She can be intimidating when she wants to be."

She hoped Clare was as sincere as she appeared. "I guess I looked a little obvious, huh?"

"We have so few VIP accounts, I think it bugged her that she didn't know about you," said Clare. "She wants to know about everything."

"Is she hard to work with?"

Clare inhaled to answer, held it, and then exhaled in resignation. She looked around, her ponytail swinging from her left shoulder to her right. No one was nearby. She said, "You can tell she's wound up tight. She's not mean exactly, just obsessed with the details." She shifted the bag of tea lights, putting her arm under it to support it. "I'm told she's changed, that she wasn't always like that. Her son died and, well, everyone assumes that's why."

A whole list of snarky comments about Lettie died on Madison's lips. She'd been so caught up in her own problems that she'd only seen Lettie as a pain in the ass. The thought of cool imperious Lettie having to deal with such grief put a different spin on things.

"I'm sorry to hear it," said Madison. "What was it, a car accident, or was he sick or something?"

"No," said Clare, looking around furtively again. "That's what's so sad. He was killed. I don't think she ever got over it. After that, she latched onto one of the employees here, defending her all the time."

"Brittany," said Madison.

Clare nodded. "I take it you've met her?"

"Oh yeah," said Madison, fearful about how much was safe to say.

"She's Brittany's champion around here. We all assume it's just pity, but who knows? Maybe Lettie can help her."

But Madison had seen how Lettie talked to Brittany in private. It was anything but warm. Yet she did defend her to Frank. It was confusing.

Smiling, Clare moved the bag to her other arm. "Well, I'd better get the tea light candles switched out. We go through a lot of them around here."

"I can see that," said Madison, marveling again at how many candles lit the pool area. "They're beautiful."

Clare elbowed Madison gently. "Don't worry about Lettie. If you have a VIP status, she'll take that seriously. The only person she protects more is Brittany."

"Thanks, I'll... have to remember that."

Clare went deeper into the pool area, swapping the burned-out tea lights for fresh ones, lighting each tiny wick before moving to the next candle.

Madison's plan to get to her cell phone was now on hold. Since Lettie rushed past the nail salon toward the locker room, there was no telling where she was right now, and Madison would rather avoid her until she'd spoken with Jason. If Lettie really was that gung-ho about defending Brittany all the time, Madison would need Jason's backup.

Meanwhile, the revelation from Clare about Lettie bothered her. Why would Lettie attach herself to a troubled girl who was so disrespectful and unhinged? Did she think of Brittany as someone she could save from herself?

She rewrapped her hair towel and left her lookout post at the entryway, walking deep into the pool area where Clare was. Standing at the beautiful long table, Clare tried to get a wick to ignite. It needed a bit of encouragement, but she soon had it lit.

"Can you tell me where the employee break room is?" asked Madison. "I need to talk to someone in there. I'll make it quick."

"Well, just don't tell anyone I told you," she said. "It's an unmarked door between the wine bar and the waxing salon."

"Thanks," said Madison, as she turned to leave. But one more thought occurred to her. "Clare, who besides Lettie or Frank can set up a VIP account?"

Clare lit the next wick. "Iris Alexander," she said. "She owns The Lazy Petal. She can do whatever she wants."

✧ ✧ ✧

ONE THING MADISON had learned over the years was that when you have to enter a room you're technically not supposed to be in, you'd better walk in like you own the joint. People assumed you had permission and were much less willing to challenge you. So she walked into the break room, head held high, passing the couches and crossing the room to where the tables and chairs were. But she discovered no amount of bluffing would fly in here today. Not when the owner was sitting right there.

And Iris had company. At her table sat Catherine Gabrielle.

Aw, crap!

They hadn't noticed her yet. Holding a cup of coffee, Iris was talking as Catherine Gabrielle nodded and wrote down what might've been instructions. She turned to a computer tablet that had a calendar on its screen. They seemed to be discussing Iris's schedule.

Gambling that confidence would get her further than meekness, she slapped a smile on her face as her eyes searched the break room for Jason. There were maybe a dozen people scattered around in matching black uniforms, while Iris and Catherine Gabrielle wore robes and hair towels. The coffee cups and snacks on the employees' tables told her there had to be food nearby, or at least a coffee pot or tea. Perhaps he was in the kitchen area?

Before Madison could nose around to find another door leading to another room, Iris noticed her and smiled. Following the direction of Iris's smile, Catherine Gabrielle turned her head. When she saw Madison, her face drooped into disapproval, sealed lips, and a slight elevation of her nose.

Madison gripped her nerve and bounced up to Iris's table, all smiles and greeting.

"Well, hello Iris!" said Madison. "Catherine Gabrielle," she nodded to Iris's assistant, who stared at Madison with an unmoving expression. "I was just looking for someone, but I'm glad to run into you. I had no idea The Lazy Petal was this fantastic! It's the most amazing spa I've ever been to."

A sniff came from Catherine Gabrielle. "And you've been to so many, have you?" she said.

Iris gave a soft chuckle. "I see you've recovered from your experience on the Ferris wheel."

"I'm still embarrassed about that," said Madison, "I'm so sorry—"

"Nonsense, we all have things we struggle with," said Iris. "No need to keep apologizing. It all turned out well and we have a nice shot we can use."

Madison pulled out a chair, sitting down at their table, while noting Catherine Gabrielle's displeasure.

"Phil wouldn't want me to say this," said Madison, "but anyone could've worn a Blue Heron costume for a lot less money. So why me? You could've had a model who wouldn't be so nervous to be at the top of a Ferris wheel."

"I'm sorry that happened," said Iris. "I didn't know you were afraid of heights. Your agent should've told me. But I think you handled yourself pretty well considering the situation."

"Phil gave me the impression that you might be disappointed."

Iris smirked and looked at her assistant. Catherine Gabrielle blushed, looking down at her notes. "I'm afraid my assistant got a little ahead of herself on that."

The assistant sat up straight and said, "I'm sorry I called your agent to complain."

In her imagination, Madison was snapping her fingers overhead in a sassy gesture while moving her head side to side, but in reality she returned a polite smile, knowing it was probably killing Catherine Gabrielle to have to apologize. "Thank you," she said. She couldn't wait to tell Spenser.

"As to why," said Iris, "it's because Veronica told me about her wonderful granddaughter. She's so proud of you." She sipped her coffee. "I had to find a model for that shoot anyway, so I decided to ask for you."

Madison looked down at the gorgeous manicure of cherry black on her fingernails, an expensive service that was free because of her VIP account. "I want to thank you for the VIP account. I understand that's also because of my grandmother."

"Same reason," said Iris. "I'm deeply grateful to Veronica. I'll let her decide how much to tell you, but I can say that because of her, many of my employees still have jobs. It was very unfortunate for the man she caught," she sighed, "but he made his own choices."

"Who was it you were looking for?" asked the assistant. Her pleasant manner didn't match the way she had regarded Madison a moment ago. "Perhaps we can help you find him."

Madison was taken aback. "How did you know it was a 'him'?"

Catherine Gabrielle's mouth barely registered a smile. "We heard there is a bit of boyfriend trouble going on."

Iris looked at her assistant with a touch of irritation. "I want you to help Madison find him."

"What?" said Madison and Catherine Gabrielle in unison, their heads swinging toward Iris.

"I think our meeting is concluded for now." Iris stood and headed for the door of the break room. "And Madison seems to need some help."

"That really won't be necessary," said Madison. "I'm fine without…"

But Iris was already through the door, closing it behind her.

Madison wondered if her own face held as much dread as Catherine Gabrielle's.

"Um…" said Madison, "let's pretend you helped me."

"Deal," said Catherine Gabrielle, a little too quickly. She looked straight ahead, struggling to maintain her business-like persona.

"So how long should we wait in here till we can walk out?"

Catherine Gabrielle seemed to consider this. "We can walk out now as long as we're together. We can split up as soon as we're sure she's not around."

"Deal," said Madison.

They cautiously stepped out the door, looking left and right. No sign of Iris. "Let's start walking," said the assistant.

Heading down the hallway, Madison decided she'd been gone from her family long enough. They'd probably already moved on to the next appointment by now, in the facials room, if her memory was right.

"Let's duck into here," said Catherine Gabrielle, turning into the pool entryway.

Madison followed. "Why in here?"

The assistant rolled her eyes. "Because the curtains are sheer and it's easier to look out into a brightly lit hallway than it is for them to look into here where the light is dim. We can watch for her. If neither of us sees her after a minute, you're free to leave."

"You mean *you're* free to leave. I'm not going to force my company on someone who hates me."

"You're the one who hates *me*," said Catherine Gabrielle.

Madison wheeled around to face her. "What? You started it."

"Excuse me? Who's the one who called me 'assistant person' as if I don't have a name?" she huffed.

"I thought that was what I was supposed to call you. Troy was saying 'person this,' and 'person that'—"

"That's how Troy talks! No one expects a genius to be polite, but normal people should be!"

"A genius damn well better be polite," said Madison, "like anyone else should be. I wasn't thinking he was a genius. I just thought he was a little… weird."

Catherine Gabrielle's shoulders dropped and she sighed. She didn't say anything, but she nodded. The women in the pool area looked at them like they were bratty toddlers in a quiet library.

Catherine Gabrielle, her voice quieter now, said, "I've always thought he was weird too."

"But Iris seemed to like him," said Madison, trying to quiet her own voice.

"Iris seems to like a lot of... challenging people," murmured the assistant.

"Don't go pointing fingers," said Madison, getting irritated again. "You fit into that category as much as anyone."

"I wasn't referring to you, but now that you mention it, you do seem determined to make my job harder!"

"Shh!"

They looked toward the pools, trying to figure out who had just shushed them.

Madison lowered her voice again. "Then who were you referring to?"

Looking annoyed, the assistant said, "Both the manager and the assistant manager here, for starters."

"Frank's not so bad when he's not mad at you. But Lettie... I don't really like her either, but I found out about her son dying and how she's never been the same. It kind of changes how you see a person, you know? I feel bad for her."

"Of course, I feel for her, too," said Catherine Gabrielle, crossing her arms in a protective gesture. "Iris feels terrible about it. But it doesn't seem smart for Iris to keep her around."

"Wow, that's pretty cold." Madison put her hands on her hips. "You think she should just fire Lettie because she's a little uptight now?"

"Don't get me wrong," she rushed to explain. "No one blames Lettie, least of all Iris. We all know it wasn't her doing, but... you'd think Lettie herself would *want* to move on. The whole thing is the ultimate in awkward situations."

"What are you talking about?"

"If Iris hadn't pressed charges, he might not have gotten himself killed in prison," said Catherine Gabrielle.

The flame of a nearby candlewick went out, while the tinkling sound of the waterfall mixed with low voices in the pool.

Rooted to her spot, Madison whispered, "The thief?" She blinked. "The man that Nika caught?"

Catherine Gabrielle nodded. "I thought you knew."

Having a clearer understanding of the dynamics between Lettie and Iris did explain at least one thing. This must be why Nika's VIP account was shrouded in mystery. Iris didn't want Lettie to find out that Nika was involved in her son's imprisonment, or that Iris was granting her a VIP account out of gratitude. For that matter, Nika already said she didn't know the assistant manager. Madison agreed: it would be best if her grandmother and Lettie knew nothing about each other.

But Brittany said that word got around and almost everyone knew about Nika. Was everyone conspiring to keep Lettie in the dark, to spare her feelings? If so, sooner or later Lettie was bound to find out.

Catherine Gabrielle kept a lookout for Iris near the main entryway while Madison kept watch at a spot near the waterfall. Peering through the sheer folds of curtains and the glass wall was not as easy as she'd thought, but she could see through them enough to keep watch. Meanwhile, from over her shoulder she could hear women in the pool nearby, discussing the loud harp music earlier.

"...jumped out of my skin. What was that about anyway?" said the first lady. Her voice was soft and delicate.

A second voice, sleepy sounding, said, "No one seems to know. Again."

The soft voice said, "The crazy stuff that goes on in this spa just keeps mounting up."

Madison resisted the urge to look over her shoulder at the ladies. She didn't want to make them feel self-conscious about her presence. She continued looking out the curtains, and listening.

A deeper womanly voice, like a sultry singer, said, "And it never feels like anyone acknowledges anything is wrong, like they don't want to admit that weird things happen here."

There was a lull in the conversation, as if that last sentence was sinking in. The harp music blended with the waterfall, masking troubled thoughts. Then the soft delicate voice said, "Remember the time we arrived and found dozens of white lilies floating in the pools?"

"I remember that," said the sultry voice. "It was pretty, but the staff seemed confused about how they got there and cleaned them all out right away."

The sleepy voice said, "I'll tell you the one that freaked me out. Remember the time someone put red lipstick on their palms and left red hand prints on the glass walls? It looked like bloody hands everywhere."

"The management continues to clean up, but not explain," said the sultry voice.

After a few minutes, Catherine Gabrielle and Madison met in the middle of the pool room. Neither of them had caught a glimpse of Iris. They concluded it was safe to part ways, if Catherine Gabrielle left first and Madison followed after a few minutes. She was anxious to get to the cell phone in her locker so she could let Jason know what was happening and ask if he had ever written down any of Brittany's past behavior. Had he ever called the police? If so, there would be a record.

Finally it was her turn to leave. But as she neared the entryway she looked up in time to see familiar pretty brown eyes coming down the hall from the direction of the locker room. Brittany wore a robe, and a head towel covered her hair. White facial cream on her cheeks covered the cut on her face.

When Madison's gaze traveled down to Brittany's deep pocket, she stopped breathing for a second. Something long and metallic, like a knife handle, peeked out at the top.

Chapter Nine

MADISON SLOWLY STEPPED back from the doorway, hoping Brittany wouldn't look inside. The sound of splashing and the peaceful voices in the pools belied her thumping heart.

A knife? Is she out of her mind? Oh yeah, we already established that.

Madison knew if she ran for help, Brittany would disappear in the maze of the spa. But she had to see where Brittany was going and make sure she didn't try to hurt anyone along the way. She waited as long as she dared, then exited the pool area.

Keeping enough distance between them to blend in with other customers, Madison watched her every move. She tried to tell herself she wasn't certain it was a knife handle. It was pretty rounded. But when she tried to imagine what else it might be, she couldn't think of anything else.

What the hell was she supposed to do if Brittany *really* went off her rocker? She was frightened to follow her, but more frightened to lose her.

Brittany approached the wine bar lounge doors, but instead of going in, she passed them, and walked further down the hallway through the curtain dividers with the Staff Only sign. Madison scurried down the length of the hallway toward those curtains. She crept up and peeked between the edges in time to see Brittany round a corner at the end of a much shorter hallway.

Madison darted into the staff area, her bare feet padding across industrial concrete. No pretty floor tiles in here. Unadorned and clinical, this part of the spa saved money on decoration by not having any. A few plain and scuffed doors lined the walls. She guessed that this was where they stored the not-so-pretty essentials like cleansers, disinfectants, or candles for the pools.

She hurried to the corner Brittany had passed, then used it for cover. Peeking around, she saw Brittany open an unmarked door.

Madison got a glimpse of the room Brittany entered. It appeared to be a supply room with a tall metal shelf filled with industrial-sized bottles of shampoo—or perhaps it was body lotion. Towers of boxes stood next to the tall shelving unit, a five-foot folding ladder leaning against one stack. Brittany dragged the ladder to the center of the room, then unfolded it and stood it up. Noticing the door was still open, she brought her foot up and kicked the door closed.

What is she doing in there?

The cold cement floor chilled her bare feet while the harp music played in the distance. *Now what? Time to tattle?* And what was she supposed to say? "Excuse me but Brittany is being bad by wearing a robe and playing on ladders." Yeah, she would lose what little credibility she had with Frank or Lettie. How do you tell people that your gut says something is wrong? People only listened to tattle tales when there was something scary to report.

Okay. She's not hurting anyone.

She felt stupid that she'd let her imagination run away with her. Just because Brittany was willing to cut her own cheek to freak out Madison didn't mean she was mental enough to start hurting random people.

She waited at that corner for what felt like an eternity, but was only a few minutes. Brittany hadn't come out. Maybe she was hiding. Maybe she was embarrassed.

There I go again assuming normal motivations for someone whose grip on reality is greased.

She needed to find Frank or Lettie and just 'fess up about everything she knew so far. She'd have to call Jason later. Brittany's behavior was just too worrisome to take any chances, and if Lettie was that concerned about Brittany all the time, she would want to know.

Madison clung to that thought. Lettie would want to know. She would approach Lettie as a concerned person who didn't want to see Brittany get into trouble. After all, Madison had taken the blame for the broken vase, hadn't she? And she was pretty sure that Lettie saw right through that at the time. So maybe she could convince Lettie to take her concerns seriously.

She turned around and headed back. First things first. She'd go in that staff door in the wine bar lounge and tell Frank what she knew.

Wait a minute. He's not here. He went to the dentist. She'd have to find Lettie.

Passing through the Staff Only curtains into the main spa, her feet back on the lovely marble floor, Madison hastened, wanting nothing more than to get this over with and to get back to her family. She'd been gone for a while now. They would definitely be wondering what kept her so long.

Nika was right. She guessed that Brittany was trouble. *She may want rope.* Madison smiled, shaking her head as she walked. It was pretty funny the way Nika could mix up American platitudes.

She came to a dead stop, staring into space. *Give her enough rope and she'll hang herself? Oh my God!*

Whirling around, she sprang back down the hallway. *Is that why she needed a ladder? To hang herself?*

Her bare feet slapped the luxury tiles as she bolted toward the supply room. Her head towel flew off as she tried to get there so fast it was yesterday. *It's all my fault! It's all my fault!*

She cursed herself for not telling the truth about Jason from the start. Her guilt dueled with her common sense. She knew that if she'd told Brittany right away, Brittany would likely have lost all her loose screws even sooner. There was no way to be certain how best to control the situation when dealing with someone like that.

Determined to get there in time to save her, she tore through the Staff Only curtains onto the crude cement floor, yelling, "I'm coming, Brittany! Hang in there!" *What the hell am I saying? Hang in there? Idiot!*

She barreled into the door, forcing it open so fast that it crashed inward and bounced back, smacking her arm and throwing her off balance. She regained her footing and stared.

Empty ladder. No Brittany.

Her breath coming fast and hard, she brushed her hair from her face. The fear in her eyes was replaced with relief. *But then, where is she?*

She stepped out of the door and looked around. No one was nearby. She looked back at the ladder standing in the center of the supply room, her gaze following its steps up. There on the ceiling was... *Is that a curling iron?*

Madison cocked her head, trying to understand. There was a curling iron clamped to what looked like a finger sized pipe coming out of the ceiling. She recognized the rounded end of the curling iron. It was what she'd seen sticking out of Brittany's pocket. The long electrical cord dangling from the curling iron led to a socket in the ceiling. A red light on the curling iron indicated it was turned on, full blast.

She stared at the ceiling pipe that the curling iron was clamped to. The relief of no hanging body gave way to the sudden revelation of what that little pipe was.

A fire alarm system.

Ah, hell!

She bolted up the ladder, reaching overhead for the curling iron. She almost had it when the alarm shattered the air with an urgent klaxon horn. Startled, Madison's hand jerked, touching the wrong end of the hot iron. A cry of pain escaped her as she lost her balance. Her arms windmilled, her foot missing a step in her panic to get down before she fell. Her feet hit the floor, dancing back a few steps, while the ladder went over with a clatter and Madison landed on her butt. The curling iron remained steadfast on the ceiling while she whipped her burned finger up and down in the air. She shoved it in her mouth to relieve the pain, and then cried out in more pain as the warmth of her tongue made it worse.

God damn that Brittany!

The alarm ripped through the hallways with its rhythmic digital grating, straining her already jangled nerves as she blew on her wet finger. Ann and Nika's relaxed bonding time was all blown to hell now.

I'm going to tattle, god damn it. I'm going to point the finger. I'll use my middle finger. I'm telling the management—No, wait! I know Iris Alexander personally. I'll tell her. That's right, Brittany. I'm going to turn your ass in to the owner of this establishment. You just wait and see if I don't.

In the back of her mind she mocked herself for her impotent rage, because in the end she knew damn well that people like Brittany didn't really care. She was the type who could fall asleep while being read the riot act.

Standing up, Madison yanked the ladder up from the floor, slamming its feet back to the center of the room. She ground her teeth, her aggravation in full flight at the lengths Brittany would go, just to ruin everyone's day.

Climbing back up the ladder, she reached for the curling iron. She was careful not to get burned this time as she unclamped it and unplugged it. The alarm continued.

Manipulative pain in the ass! Let's see her manipulate the management when I tell them who's responsible…

Her thoughts were interrupted by a woman's loud, stern voice from the base of the ladder, trying to be heard over the alarm. "What are you doing in here? You should be vacating along with—"

Madison whipped her head around and saw Lettie standing just inside the doorway. Lettie cut off her own sentence when her eyes went from the curling iron in

Madison's hand to the little pipe on the ceiling. Lifting her chin as if being confronted with a challenge, she seemed to be declaring, rather than asking…

"You set off the alarm?"

"What?" said Madison, incredulous. "No! I was—"

"Madison Cruz. Our new VIP."

Madison winced. "Well… kind of, but—"

Into a cell phone, Lettie said, "I found her. It looks like she's the one who set off the alarm."

"It wasn't me!" Madison scurried down the ladder, keeping the curling iron at a safe angle.

The alarm grated on.

"Stay away from me," said Lettie, backing up, watching the curling iron as if it were a weapon.

"I'm not the problem," said Madison, pleading. "It's Brittany. She's banana bread!"

"Brittany went home," said Lettie. "Her shift is over."

"But I *saw her*," Madison insisted. "She came in here!"

Lettie looked Madison up and down, seeming to come to a decision. "The whole place is in a panic. The decent thing would be for you to help me shut off the alarm."

"I'd *love* to shut it off, but I don't know how!"

"Frank has the code, but he's not here," said Lettie. She looked at the ceiling. "We'll have to do it at the source, where it went off."

Madison looked at the ceiling, confused. "But—"

"Stay here," Lettie said. "Please tell any employees that come by that it's a false alarm and that I'm getting the external key. You get on the ladder, and I'll pass it up to you. Your young knees can handle that ladder better than mine. It's the least you can do after all this." She about-faceed, and hurried out the door.

She thinks I did it. This can't be happening! She had to explain to Lettie and make her understand.

She ran into the hall, her bare feet cold on the concrete floor, but Lettie was already out of sight. As Madison hurried to catch up with her, she heard something from behind.

Looking over her shoulder she caught a glimpse of Brittany's hands gripping a huge vase as it rushed down toward Madison's head.

Chapter Ten

HER HANDS FLEW up to protect herself as she spun, hunching her shoulders and ducking her head. The impact of the vase sounded like an explosion, up close and personal. Her hands took the painful brunt of the blow, lessening the impact on her head, but she still felt the shock. She had a fleeting realization that the curling iron was still miraculously in her hand. A surge of adrenaline turned her grip to iron.

"You're trying to ruin everything!" screamed Brittany.

Madison felt sharp pieces grazing her forehead and eyelids as shattered ceramic rained down her face. Brittany shoved her, and the shock that she was actually being attacked helped her to rally.

"What's the matter with you?" cried Madison, blinded from the debris on her face. Her left hand rushed to her eyes as she struck out with the curling iron, swinging it hard, blindly hitting something solid. A pained grunt burst from Brittany. Madison swung the curling iron again in a backhand, slamming it into the girl.

Brittany tried to take the curling iron but accidently grabbed the hot end and cried out, letting go immediately. "I hate you!" she shouted, swinging her fists at Madison.

Madison slashed the curling iron back and forth to fend off her attacker. She ran her left forearm over her brows and eyelids in an effort to clear away the powdered debris, while she blew out her nose and spit pieces that had stuck on her lips. Her violent blinking returned some sight to her, enabling a better aim. "Grow the fuck up, Brittany!" she shouted.

Brittany yanked the curling iron out of her hand by the dangling wire. As it fell to the ground, the wire tangled their feet while Brittany reached up for two handfuls of Madison's dark hair.

Madison instinctively brought the heel of her left fist down hard on Brittany's face, embarrassed that she was hitting like a girl, but hey, from one girl to another... *Take that you crazy bitch!* The fist landed hard and squarely on Brittany's nose, producing an angry squeal. At the same time Madison's right fist swung into the side of Brittany's head.

With Madison's hair firmly in her hands, Brittany wrenched Madison's head downward and side to side while she shouted, "You took him, you bitch!"

It was happening so fast that Madison marveled she had enough presence of mind to form a hard fist with her right hand and punch up into Brittany's throat.

The blow cut off her words, and she let go of Madison's hair with a gurgling sound. With one hand holding her throat, she placed a foot on Madison's hip and shoved hard, throwing her to the ground. But before Madison could get to her feet, Brittany ran down the hallway in the opposite direction from where Lettie had gone.

Trying to stand, Madison struggled with the curling iron cord that had tangled her feet, and finally kicked it aside. She shook her head to clear the fog, pieces of the vase flying out of her hair. Brittany's attack couldn't have lasted a whole minute, but the fear and adrenaline reminded her of fending off bullies in grade school, and she deeply resented being forced to feel twelve years old again. Yet, instead of feeling even more angry after this attack, she was sobered by a realization.

Brittany wasn't just crazy. She was dangerous.

And now Miss Danger Nut was somewhere in the catacombs of these back rooms. But it didn't matter where. Getting hit over the head made Madison realize with a panic where Jason might be. Earlier, Brittany said that Jason owed her his job, and that the last wine server *(was it Barry?)* had "hurt his little head," a dismissive way of saying the poor guy was injured so badly he had to leave his job.

It wasn't likely Brittany would be able to hit Jason on the head with a wine bottle—unless he didn't see it coming. Like Barry, perhaps?

The alarm grated on.

She ran through the Staff Only curtains, her fear for Jason making the fight feel less important.

Jason! Damn me, I should've realized sooner!

The relaxed atmosphere of the spa had disappeared. Stragglers in the hallways argued with employees about whether there was any real danger, assuming this was another prank. Some were angry, reluctant to go outside in their robes, resisting the employees in black uniforms who were guiding, beckoning, or even herding everyone toward the front lobby exit. Madison ignored them, intent on heading into the wine bar.

Then a loud but low-pitched boom hit her ears, making her whole body jump. A second boom sounded. It reminded her of illegal firecrackers, cherry bombs that boys would throw into the girls' restroom as a prank during her school days. It was quite effective then. It was quite effective now.

Panic filled The Lazy Petal. She heard a few screams, and in the distance she saw women rush out of the pool doors holding robes hastily closed over their wet bodies, trailing water across the floor. Some ran out nude in their panic, trying to wrap towels around themselves as they went. They may not have believed there was an emergency before, but they believed it now.

Why would Brittany have cherry bombs? It didn't add up. *Do crazy people come prepared in case they get in the mood to let their hair down and go all nutball?*

The rhythmic grating horn of the alarm was now joined by a recorded male voice. "Please vacate the building... Please vacate the building..."

Madison hated knowing that all these poor women were terrified by a false alarm. She wanted to assure them that everything was all right, but she had to get to Jason first. He was the only one who might be seriously hurt.

"...Please vacate the building..."

Lettie rushed up to her, holding a ring of keys. "Here's the external key."

Madison put on the brakes to keep from mowing her down. She also put her hands up in front of her to plead. "Please Lettie, I don't have time! I think Jason is behind those curtains in the wine bar, seriously hurt. He needs our help!"

"He's already been found and medics were called," said Lettie quickly. Putting her hands on Madison's shoulders, she added, "Don't worry, he's all right. Just a little bruising. But how did you know about it?"

"Brittany snuck up behind me and hit me over the head with a vase! We fought and—"

"She came back to the supply room?" said Lettie, looking grave.

"Yes, that's what I'm trying to tell you! She—"

"We have to hurry," said Lettie. "People are panicking and getting hurt. We have to shut off this alarm."

"But, you're sure he's—"

"...Please vacate the building..."

"Please!" said Lettie, "I need your help."

"All right. Let's go." She ran back toward the storage room, Lettie keeping up with her.

They ran through the Staff Only curtains.

That's why Brittany had wine all over her clothes.

They ran toward the storage room.

I should've realized it when he wasn't at the wine bar counter, and Lettie ran in, turning down the volume...

She stopped just inside the supply room, and that's when it hit her. She slowly turned her head to look at Lettie. She felt sick as realization sunk in on her.

She looked behind the wine bar curtains and didn't say a word.

"Relax," said Lettie. "I'm going to fix everything." She shoved Madison hard with surprising strength. Madison tripped backward, crashing into the ladder.

Lettie slammed the door shut as Madison scrambled to regain her balance. A frantic clicking and snap from the doorknob told Madison she was being locked in. She flew at the door, trying to turn the knob, furious at herself for believing that key was to turn off the alarm.

"Why?" Madison yelled. "It doesn't make sense!" She yanked at the knob. "Let me out!"

"…Please vacate the building…"

"Lettie!" Madison pounded on the door. "Lettie, what do you know about Jason?" She tried to be heard over the grating horn, the recorded voice, and through a door. She pounded again.

"Lettie? Lettie, talk to me. Please!" She got down on the floor, trying to look under the door. Just the barest of space between the door and the floor, but it was enough to show her that Lettie was already gone.

She sat up, staring at the door in disbelief. A school yard fight with the resident drama queen, and now this? *What the hell is going on?*

If Jason really was behind that curtain in the wine bar, then he must have been unconscious when Lettie looked back there. So why would she lie to Frank and say she didn't know where he was? But if he wasn't back there, why would she lie and say he'd already been found? Worse, if he really was back there when she looked, she was cold hearted enough to leave him injured without any help. What could she possibly gain from letting him stay there, unattended to, maybe losing blood?

Well, Madison damn sure wasn't going to stay in this room and wait on Lettie's pleasure. She had to get out of there, fast. *Come on, Madison! Think like a spy. It's in your blood. What would Mom do? Or Nika?*

Tearing through the supplies on the shelves, she inspected any container or box that might hold tools. One box had a small broken coffee maker, a few spoons, napkins, and coffee mugs, and a moldy piece of birthday cake that had more green and gray fuzzy spots than icing. The mold had spread up the side of the box. *Disgusting!*

Other boxes had candles, spare light bulbs, cleansers, and more of those complimentary jars of mud. Her heart sank.

She had to at least try to use what she'd found.

Grabbing a spoon and a coffee mug, she set to work to remove the hinge pins on the door. She'd seen Grandpa do this before, but he used a hammer and punch. She hoped her spoon and mug would suffice.

Starting with the hinge in the middle, she set the narrow end of the spoon at its base. Using the bottom of the coffee mug like a hammer, she pounded upward on the wide end of the spoon. The hinge didn't budge for the few first blows, but then it started to move. Thrilled, she frantically hit upward on the spoon, watching the hinge rise but also seeing the spoon bend further and further out of shape until it was useless. Throwing it aside, she grabbed another spoon out of the box, pounding upward again.

The hinge popped out! It had taken less than a minute. Elated, she hurried to the next hinge at the top of the door. She pounded upward, but this one didn't want to budge. Her fear of failure made her frantic, and she swung the coffee mug off center, grazing fingers already sore from her earlier encounter with Brittany and the vase.

Then, the lights went out.

She froze, holding her breath.

"…Please vacate the building…"

"I get it already!" she yelled into the dark. "Shut up!" But the alarm continued to wear down her composure. She was angry that darkness could have such an effect on her. She felt like a child.

Her eyes not yet used to the dark, all she saw was black; not even a shape or a glimmer. Nothing. As much as she tried to deny her fear, her heart pounded, accusing her of being inadequate.

Refusing defeat, she resumed pounding upward in the dark, her aim poor. Her fear rose again, making her pound as hard as she could, shattering the mug. A cry escaped her throat.

Moving across the floor in a slow gliding motion, she pushed aside broken pieces of the mug with her bare feet. Feeling around in the dark, relief flooded her when she found the box again, recognizing it by the feel of the broken coffee maker inside. Impatiently, she plunged her hand in to grab another mug and instead got a handful of moldy cake. Yanking her hand out, she whipped it to the side, wondering where the gross cake was landing in the dark. She shoved her hand back in, moving it around to find the other mug. *Where is it? Damn it!* Her eyes stung with tears, which only made her more frantic as she rummaged in the box, until her fingers touched something hard. She felt its shape. *Oh my god. A hammer! Yes!*

The hammer made short work of the hinge, destroying her last spoon in the process, but the hinge was out. *Mom and Nika would be proud!* They were probably outside with Spenser in the parking lot, looking for her among the crowd. It wouldn't occur to them that she was still inside.

She didn't need the final hinge at the bottom of the door to come out. Using the claw of the hammer, she pulled the top portion of the door toward her, just enough to get a grip and yank it sideways about an inch. The latch escaped the door frame and the door swung open.

Thankfully, there was a little more light in the hallway as she carefully made her way in the dark, silently trotting for the Staff Only curtains.

The alarm continued to honk, and the recorded voice made a pest of itself with its repeated warning. Madison wondered how long the alarm had been going now. Seven minutes? Ten? So much had happened in such a short amount of time. But shouldn't fire engines or some other emergency response be arriving by now?

Cautiously poking her head out of the curtains, she saw that the way to the wine bar doors was clear, but she'd need to be careful and stick to the shadows. Spots of light illuminated bits of the hallway where candles still burned, their small brightness set on tables or emanating from within a few salon doorways. She could see up ahead that the pool entryway in particular had some glow about it.

Two figures stood at the entryway to the pool area. Madison crept up the hallway, staying close to the wall, trying to reach the doors to the wine bar. As she got to the doors and slowly pushed them open, she realized that the figures at the pool entryway were Lettie and Brittany.

Even over the alarm, Madison could hear the loud smack as Lettie slapped Brittany, yelling, "If you don't quit your sick little dramas and stick to the plan I will tell your mother about Barry! Don't think I won't!"

Madison slipped through the doors.

Chapter Eleven

"It's because you got hit on your head," said Madison. "But how long do you think you've been awake?"

No answer. As she'd suspected, Jason was in the small curtained room behind the wine bar. In the dim light, she could see him blinking. His awareness seemed to come and go.

Kneeling next to him, she tenderly felt around his face, finding a sizable goose egg on his forehead. Examining the cut on his scalp, she figured a blow to the back of his head caused him to collapse forward and hit his forehead on the floor. She'd found him sitting up in the dark, a cork in his hand, a forgotten towel in his lap, and a puddle of wine on the floor. The sweet pungent scent filled the room, and broken wine bottles like carcasses were scattered as if a case of wine had fallen from a high shelf.

"Ow," he said, pulling his face away. He sounded groggy.

She patted his hand and kissed it, noting it was sticky. She couldn't tell if it was dried wine, or dried blood.

She looked around. At least it wasn't quite as dark as the supply room had been, but it was still a little tricky to know what she was seeing. A black door shape in the back wall gave her hope. She stood up and slowly walked to it, putting her hands out to see what she'd touch. It was a doorway all right, and because her hands passed through it, it must be open. She'd much rather go out in this direction than back into the wine bar lobby where Lettie or Brittany might see them and try to stop them. She didn't know her way around back there, but Jason would, if he could get his senses back in time.

Again Jason asked, "Why am I in bed?" This worried Madison. She'd already explained to him that he wasn't in bed, that he was on the floor in the wine bar at The Lazy Petal.

"…Please vacate the building…"

"The TV's too loud," he mumbled.

Squatting, she placed her hand on his cheek. "That's an alarm, and although you really should be in bed, you're not. You're sitting on the floor in—"

"Madison." He'd said it as if she'd just walked in.

"Yes," she said, smiling in the dark. "That's right. I'm Madison.

"You'd better get behind me," he said, woozy.

"What?"

"I think someone hit me. They might come back," he said, trying to stand. She wrapped her arms around his shoulders, trying to steady him.

"And you're going to protect me, huh?"

"Hell yeah," he said, his voice weak and sleepy.

She stifled a giggle even as tears threatened. Obviously he'd suffered a bad concussion and was in a vulnerable state. She had to get him out of there before he started throwing punches at shadows, or worse, causing himself another blow to his head.

She lifted his arm to drape around her shoulders, wrapping her arm around his waist. "We have to leave," she said. "Hold on tight." Helping him support his weight proved to be a bigger challenge than she'd thought.

Navigating Jason's lumbering gait through the wine bottles on the floor, she led them out of the dark room into an equally dark service hallway. She was sure this hallway led to the hallway where she'd been locked in a supply room. This whole labyrinth of service hallways had to be connected, and had to have other exit doors where delivery trucks could drop off shipments of supplies. She just needed to find one.

Hey! Why haven't I seen any illuminated exit signs? There was nothing, as if all of their emergency batteries were dead. Or removed?

The annoying alarm continued, making her wonder why the fire department hadn't arrived yet. Hadn't they been called?

Then she realized, no. No, of course not. Lettie had some other reason for wanting this place empty, and she'd used Brittany to do it. Who knows what story she'd cooked up for the patrons outside?

"Where's the nearest exit?" she asked him.

No answer. He didn't seem to know she was there, even though she was helping him stay upright. Jason shouldn't be moving at all, but she couldn't let them be found. She still didn't understand what this was about, and Lettie might have a reason to want to hurt them or stop them from leaving. She had to be careful. Maybe she should park him somewhere safe while she looked for an exit.

The shadows along the wall of the concrete hallway indicated large shelving units. With one arm firmly around his waist, she used the other hand to quickly feel the shelves, confirming that they were just like the ones in the supply room where the alarm went off. Was that a rolled up blanket on the bottom shelf?

Slowing, she said, "Let's stop here. I want you to sit on the floor. We'll go slow. Ready?"

"You have a sexy voice."

Trying to ignore that, she repeated, "Real slow. Are you ready?"

"Why are my pants wet?"

"You were sitting in wine," she said. "Now let's sit down, okay?"

No answer.

"Okay?" she repeated. "Jason, do you hear me?"

"Let's go back to bed," he said.

"Jason, we're not..."

"Jason doesn't feel right," he said.

"Of course you don't, you poor baby. You got hit on..."

"No, I mean Jason. Are you sure that's my name?"

After a moment she tried to make her voice sound calm "Yes. You're Jason Clark. My grandfather knows your grandfather, remember? They've been friends for years."

Silence.

"Don't worry," she patted him, trying to make it sound like everything was fine. "It'll all come back soon." But in her heart she was worried sick at how disoriented he was.

It wasn't exactly graceful, but she got him down to the floor without any sudden bumps.

"I'm so tired," he said, half asleep.

Those three simple words broke her heart. He was displaying all the classic symptoms of a bad concussion, and he didn't deserve one. He'd just wanted to end the day peacefully. He'd tried to warn her about Brittany, and she thought he was exaggerating. Yes, she'd felt guilty about not telling Brittany that they were dating, but the truth was that it was none of Brittany's business who he wanted to date, ever. She had no right to hurt him like this.

"Sit here for a minute," she said, trying to keep the fear out of her voice. "I have to move some boxes."

From the bottom shelf, she pulled three heavy boxes out onto the floor. The sound of cardboard sliding across a cement floor filled the space as she quickly shoved them away from the shelving unit so she could pull out the rolled up carpet or blanket that she'd found back there. She spread it out on the floor for him.

"Jason, there's a nice space near you that you can lie down on." In the darkness, she looked where she'd left him sitting, but he wasn't there. "Jason?"

"…Please vacate the building…"

He was walking down the hallway.

"Jason," she called. She didn't know if he could hear her over the alarm. Running up to him, she said, "Where are you going?"

"I'm done with the car," he said.

"That's… that's good. I'm glad," she said, putting her hands on his arms to turn him the other way.

Right then, the alarm stopped. Dead silence in the hallway. Immense relief that the damn thing had stopped poured through her, but the silence led her to the question of why. Why had it stopped, and why now?

Peering at the ceiling in the dark, Madison tried to figure out if she was hearing something, or if the alarm had left her ears ringing. Jason had brought his hands up to her head, so it was difficult to tell.

"I've always loved your hair," he said, his voice alluring and sexy. He pulled her into his arms and kissed her like he meant business. He may have been drowsy, but she was caught off guard by how firmly he held her. And by... other... firm things.

"Whoa, whoa," she said, gently pulling back. "You know I love that, but this isn't the—"

He cut off her words in a burst of haste, kissing her again with insistence, his strong arms pulling her up, her toes barely touching the floor.

"Mmff... Jas... mmff..."

She tried getting his attention by lightly slapping his shoulders, afraid of touching anywhere on his injured head. "Mmff... stop," she said, pulling her face away.

"Tiffany, please."

"*What?*"

"Right now," he said with some urgency.

"I..." She swallowed her pride. "Look, we have to get out of here. Where's the nearest exit?"

His hands began to help themselves, with passion and purpose.

"Jason," she said, slapping his hands from her breasts. "Try to think, because we need—" He moved his hands to her ass. She reached around, grabbing his wrists, pulling his hands away. "What's gotten into you? We have to go…" He nibbled on her ear, his tongue trailing down her neck while one hand pulled at her robe tie.

"For God's sake, Jason, I"—a sharp inhale—"I'm only human," she said, trying to control herself and catch her breath. She pushed him away and he staggered drunkenly. Fear seized her and she lunged forward in a panic, wrapping her arms around him, holding him upright.

"Oh god, I shouldn't have pushed you, I'm so sorry."

"Chelsea," he said, "I don't feel so good." His head hung and his shoulders slouched like he was getting sleepy again. He brought his hand to his face.

Madison heard distant voices echoing in the hallway. They were getting closer. Lettie and Brittany sounded like they were arguing. Madison walked Jason as quickly as she could into the nearest supply room, hoping Jason wouldn't stumble in the dark and fall or make noise.

She closed the door quietly, her fear growing.

"What's going on?" he mumbled.

"I need you to be really quiet, now." She lowered him into an empty corner of the room. A stack of big boxes in front of him would hide him if they opened the door. She kissed him lightly and whispered, "Try to go to sleep, okay?" He didn't answer. She hoped it was because he was actually going to sleep.

She could still hear them arguing in the distance. Getting up, she looked around in the dim light, desperate to find something she could use as a weapon, just in case. She found a wrench sitting on a shelf, took it, and settled herself down behind the boxes next to Jason. On her toes, she leaned forward onto her knees, resting her weight up on her heels, both hands clutching the wrench in front of her, keeping him behind her. If they were discovered, she already knew Brittany wanted to seriously hurt her, and maybe Lettie would help. Madison might have to take on two women at once, and she didn't really know how to fight. She was a girly-girl; always had been. But she also knew that fighting involved the right attitude, and she would do whatever she had to, to protect herself and Jason.

No more fighting like a girly-girl. No more holding back, afraid to actually hurt someone. Lettie and Brittany had raised the stakes, not her. She was ready to fight like a demon. *Yeah, that's it!* She liked this thought pattern. *Keep thinking like that.* She would sure surprise them, all right. They'd be sorry if they tried anything.

As she steeled herself…

I'll kick their asses!

…and tried to pep talk herself into being an Action Gal superhero…

They won't know what hit them! I'll... I'll...

...her eyes flew open as Jason, showing no hesitancy whatsoever, slipped his hand under her robe and between her legs. The unexpected pleasure shocked her.

In an urgent whisper, she choked out, "Are you crazy?" She tried to twist away, slapping at his hand, losing the wrench, and lost her precarious balance when he pulled her toward him. He had her in his lap looking up at him, his hand behind her head, his other hand at work under her robe, as he kissed her mouth, pressing into her lips. *What the hell?* She squirmed, trying to be gentle with him, pulling his hand away, trying to close her legs, and turn her face away. He had never, ever, acted like this before. "Not *now*," she pleaded, trying to sit up, trying to be sensible, wishing she didn't have to be.

"You're confusing," he said, nibbling her ear again, reaching deep in her robe to resume his silky work.

"You have to stop," she whispered, hanging on to his forearm between her knees—but not quite pushing him away now. She marveled that he could get her aroused so quickly. It must be her nerves, she told herself.

"Why?" he said, still working under her robe as he murmured in her ear. "Don't you like it?"

Does a hungry girl want her cookies?

Pushing his hand away while sitting up, in a panicked whisper she said, "Okay, okay, I'll make you a deal. Am I Tiffany? Chelsea? Whoever you want, Jason, just not right now, okay? If you're quiet and don't touch me, I'll be whoever you want later. Just *please* be quiet."

"That's not funny, Elena," he said. "Who's Tiffany?"

She looked at him in the dark, her mouth hanging open. "Uh... tell you later? I think?" she whispered in her best attempt to placate him. "But let's be really, really quiet now, okay?"

The tragedy was knowing he had a nice firm package there. *But apparently it's not for me.* And she knew that even if it *were* for her instead of Tiffany, or Chelsea, or Elena, or whoever the hell else he had in his horny little mind, there wasn't a damn thing she could do about it. She shook her head hard, taking deep breaths, trying to shake off the state he'd put her in. *Dammit!* She needed to concentrate. They were still in danger and she needed to be ready.

She listened, but couldn't pick up any voices through the closed door.

She whispered, "We might get killed if I don't find us a way out of here."

"Well, why didn't you say so?" he said, in a sleepy mumble. "There's an exit nearby in this hallway," he murmured as he leaned into the corner, closing his eyes.

Now you tell me.

The voices started up again, getting closer. *They're here.*

As the voices came nearer, Madison could make out their words. Lettie said, "What are you doing now? I need you to help me carry this."

Brittany's voice came from a little further away. "I just want to see him."

"You don't have to gloat over him. We have to do this fast."

"But—"

"He isn't going anywhere!" Lettie snapped. "Now come on. We have to hurry."

Madison could hear the sound of boxes being pushed across the floor, and cardboard tearing as if the lids of boxes were being opened.

"Don't give me that look," said Lettie "You said he was dead."

"I just let you think he was dead," said Brittany. "I wouldn't kill my honey. He wants me."

"He looked pretty dead to me," said Lettie. "But it doesn't matter."

"What do you mean? Of course it matters."

Lettie's voice took on a much friendlier tone, as if she were talking to a child. "I'm sorry, sweetheart. What I meant was, soon you'll be the assistant manager, and if he's alive like you say, he'll be pretty impressed when he wakes up, don't you think? That's why you don't want to wake him just yet. Do you understand?"

A petulant sigh from Brittany. "All right. But I get to be the one to wake him."

"Of course," said Lettie.

"And don't you slap me again. You think my mom will get mad if you tell her about Barry? Just wait till I tell her you slapped me. She'll fire you."

Madison closed her eyes, annoyed with herself for not spotting the obvious. Iris Alexander employed her own crazy daughter, and although Iris knew it was a challenge for Frank, she made them take Brittany on.

"Relax," said Lettie. "I'm going to fix everything."

Madison had heard that before. Lettie had said it just before she locked Madison in the supply room.

Chapter Twelve

SHE HEARD THEM walking away, complaining about who was carrying the heaviest box. She waited another minute before carefully opening the door and peering into the hallway. All clear. She stepped out.

Jason had fallen asleep in the corner of the supply room. That seemed about as safe as any place she could think of for him. But she couldn't wait to talk to a doctor and find out if increased sexual drive was one of the possible symptoms of a bad concussion. She'd heard that some people didn't act like themselves while their brains were healing, but *come on!* Confusing people's names was one thing, but holy crap! He'd made more moves on her in the last few minutes than he had in the last few weeks. She dared not tell her mom, who knew his family. Spenser would be beside herself laughing, teasing Madison for not going for it.

She ran up and down the hallway, looking for the exit door he'd said was near the supply room they were hiding in. When she finally found it, it was locked. It was sinking in that the whole place must have been locked up, and maybe that was why no one had come in to help. Locked doors, no more alarm, no lights, and obviously no fire. Just a bunch of women in robes, stranded in the parking lot. What possible goal could Lettie and Brittany have in mind?

Well, there was one thing they may have forgotten. The front door of the check-in lobby was glass. If Madison could sneak into the lobby, she'd be able to see the others in the parking lot and wave them over to the door. She could yell for them to call the police and an ambulance.

She could also try to sneak into the locker room and get her cell phone to make the calls herself. The locker room and front lobby check-in were right next to each other. So the question was, which method would be the fastest to get the help they needed?

As she hurried through the dark, she kept her hands in front of her, feeling for obstacles in her way. She'd figured out that these back hallways were mostly connected, and this was how employees got around, delivered supplies, went on lunch breaks, all without the patrons ever seeing the mundane happenings behind the scenes. It helped sustain the illusion that The Lazy Petal was a wonderland of relaxation. But after hearing the women in the pool earlier talking about all the strange occurrences, and after experiencing this insane day, she doubted that Iris would be able to keep all of her clients.

Many would desert The Lazy Petal for some rival spa because they no longer felt secure here. Luxury wasn't worth it if you had to keep looking over your shoulder.

She found the connecting hallway that led to the original supply room she'd been locked in, and from there she found the curtains that led to the marble tiled hallway. She was back where she'd first followed Brittany through the Staff Only curtain, but at least now she knew her way.

Heading in the direction of the check-in lobby where the front door was located, she tried to run silently on her bare toes, careful not to let the slap of feet on marble tiles alert anyone to her presence. She hurried along the hallway, trying to avoid the spots of soft illumination where doors stood open, the ghostly glow of candlelight emanating from within. She may not know what Lettie and Brittany were up to, but she had no doubt they would try to stop her from getting outside if they saw her. Lettie had proven that by leaving her locked in a supply room, and leaving Jason for dead.

At that moment the scent of cherry blossoms filled the hallway, reminding her of the massage she and Spenser had enjoyed earlier. It seemed an odd smell, here and now. She heard voices and came to a stop. She crouched in the dark, trying to keep her breathing quiet.

Of all the doorways, the pool entryway up ahead had the brightest glow coming out of it, although she would hardly call it bright. Besides voices, she heard splashing, but it sounded wrong. It wasn't the delicate splash of the waterfall anymore. It sounded more like a bucket of slop hitting the flat surface of the water.

A few more careful steps and she'd be on the edge of the entryway. She hoped to pass it undetected. Then she could make a break for it and run to the front check-in lobby before Brittany, who was probably the faster of the two, could stop her.

She got down on her hands and knees and peered around the edge of the pool entryway. The gauzy curtains provided a bit of cover, but they also made it difficult to see where Brittany and Lettie were. She heard another plop of liquid. The scent of cherry blossoms was powerful.

"This part still doesn't make sense to me," said Brittany. "We're not ruining the pool area. We're just making it messy. It won't be hard for them to clean it up."

"It's not the clean up, dear. It's for ruining the waterfall," said Lettie. "We'll be able to get a brand new one, won't that be nice? A bigger, more beautiful waterfall."

"But I don't care about the waterfall," said Brittany.

"Once Frank is fired for this fiasco and I'm manager, I'll be able to help you like I promised. So think of the waterfall as my reward," said Lettie.

"I still don't see the point."

"You don't need to. You just need to trust me. It's finally all about to get fixed."

Madison backed up from the entryway, sitting on the floor and leaning against the wall. Her heart pounded. Taking some calming breaths, she dropped her head down into her hands and tried to think. Lettie and Brittany thought Madison was still locked away in that supply room, so they wouldn't be expecting her right now. She needed to decide if she should risk trying to quietly sneak past the entryway, or if she should just run for it. They would no doubt see her through either the entryway or through the glass walls, but would they be able to stop her before she could make it to the front lobby? Before she could pound on the glass door to get the attention of the patrons outside?

"Why am I not surprised?" said Lettie. Madison snapped her head up to see Lettie standing in front of her. How had she walked up so quietly?

"How'd you get out?" asked Brittany, standing off to the side. Madison looked back and forth at each of them, trying to calculate their intentions.

"It doesn't matter," said Lettie. "I was coming to let her out right now."

"You were?" said Brittany. Madison held still, not trusting anything either of them had to say. She slowly stood up, looking at their hands for any sign of a weapon.

Lettie smiled, and Madison had the feeling that her smile itself was indeed a weapon.

"I know this looks bad to you," said Lettie. "But I'm hoping you'll hear me out. Come into the pool room where we can all see better."

Madison was standing now, but uncertain about her next move. Brittany wore her petulant expression again, looking at the floor as if she'd lost a coin toss or an argument. The white cream on her face was long gone. The red cut down her cheek that made her look so fierce and scary earlier seemed to diminish her now, as if her wound displayed much deeper troubles within. The contrast with those pretty brown eyes was heartbreaking. Madison watched her walk back into the pool entryway.

Lettie was standing some distance from Madison, watching her with a mild expression. "Well?" she said. "Will you give me a chance to explain?" She held her arm out toward the pool entryway, and then walked in first, giving Madison the choice to follow or turn and run.

So she followed.

The pool area was indeed better lit than the rest of the deserted spa, all its candles still burning. She saw empty boxes in the back corners, and empty plastic gallon-sized bottles littered all over the ground. One pool, the largest one, had a colorful sheen, almost rainbow-like, floating in patches on the surface where Lettie and Brittany must've poured cherry blossom oil. What a mess. Another scent assaulted her nose. Was it nail polish? Madison looked for signs of nail polish color, but couldn't see any.

"It's been a difficult year for Brittany and me. Her, with her mother constantly trying to run her life and keep tabs on everything she does, even down to her day job here at The Lazy Petal. Isn't that right, dear?" She inclined her head toward Brittany.

Brittany pouted, watching Madison from under her brows. "I'm going to be assistant manager here," she said. She lifted her chin, and for a moment she again resembled the capable young woman Madison had seen in the nail salon earlier. It seemed the poor girl was at war with herself, her petulant side at odds with the young adult trying to find her way in the world. Her mental instability added an extra burden to the already difficult task of trying to grow up.

Standing near the table with folded towels, Madison decided to play along. "And why is that? Lettie is the assistant manager here."

"Because Frank is stupid," said Brittany. "He doesn't like me and he doesn't have the right to not like me. My mother owns The Lazy Petal and that means I'll be the owner some day. So he has to go."

"Okay," Madison said carefully. "So how are you getting rid of him? Did you ask your mother to fire him?"

Brittany snorted her laughter. "Right. As if she'd ever listen to me." She shook her head as if Madison were clueless.

Lettie poured one last plastic gallon jug of cherry blossom oil all over the waterfall.

Brittany straightened her posture and said, "We're giving her a little help with the decision. We're showing her how badly he's prepared the place for an emergency. Not even the fire department is responding. What if this had been a real emergency? He failed. That's not how a manager does his job."

"You mean you made it *look* like he failed," said Madison.

Brittany looked at Lettie. "Lettie will be the new manager, and since she can hire who she wants, she's going to hire me."

Madison said nothing. Lettie was using Brittany, that much was obvious, but it was such a transparent sham that there was no way they could get away with it. So if they couldn't get away with it, the real goal was something else.

"Lettie," said Madison, "Are you willing to tell me why you did this in the middle of a business day? With lots of patrons being herded out into the parking lot?"

Lettie surveyed the state of the pool room and sighed at her handiwork. "All those traumatized women." She sounded peaceful. "Rich people love to sue. Iris may be in litigation hell for years after this. At least, I hope so."

"Jason won't want you anymore," Brittany cut in, causing Lettie to roll her eyes. "He was probably just using you because I was gone for a while."

"Yeah, and how's he going to feel knowing you clobbered him with a wine bottle?" asked Madison.

Brittany didn't say anything. Instead she shot a glance at Lettie.

Lettie smiled and said, "Don't look at me, I didn't say anything." She walked to the front table, straightening towels.

"And what about Barry?" asked Madison. "Do you feel any remorse for him at all?"

Brittany stared at her, wide eyed, but Lettie laughed. "Can you believe it? She actually used the identical attack, like no one would put it together."

Brittany whipped her head in Lettie's direction, incredulous. "Lettie…"

Lettie picked up a towel and stepped up to the sliding glass entryway, wiping it down, making it perfect as she said, "My year has been difficult too. Having to be in the company with the piece of shit that sent my son to prison." She turned to face Madison. "And having to work with her offspring, knowing that my own offspring was dead."

Ignoring Lettie, Brittany asked, "Does Jason know?" She seemed agitated, as if this possibility had just occurred to her. "Does he know it was me?"

"Brittany," said Madison. "Do you care only about whether he knows it was you? Aren't you worried about how badly he's injured?"

Brittany's face was blank, as if she didn't understand the question.

Madison told Lettie, "You know Iris must love her and can afford the best of care for her. Have you been trying to sabotage her treatments? Talking her into skipping medication or something?"

With a kilowatt smile that approached pageant levels, Lettie's face held far more satisfaction than she had shown before. Madison had her answer.

Brittany screamed at Madison with no distinct words, grabbing a glass tea light holder. Still holding it, she smashed its edge on the floor, breaking the edges into sharp points. "You think you know everything," she yelled. "I'm going to carve up your ugly face."

"Oh no," said Madison as her shoulders slumped. "Do we have to fight again? Don't you ever get enough drama?"

Raising the jagged glass into the air, she ran at Madison.

Stunned that this girl never got enough, she was determined this time to show Brittany that the cost would be too great. Crazy or not, most people at least understand pain.

Madison snatched a towel from the table just as Brittany bore down on her. As the sharp glass swung at her, she caught Brittany's hand in the towel, wrapping it in a split second and yanking the glass out of her hand and into the towel. She felt the back of her hair being pulled down, forcing her to look upward. She couldn't see to aim, but she swung her fist and slugged Brittany's nose just as in their earlier fight. The impact had the desired effect of shocking her with pain. She let go of Madison's hair, covering her nose with her hands. Madison was deeply grateful that that was all it took to get a brief advantage over Brittany, but she had to move fast if she wanted to be the one to dominate before Brittany attacked again.

With the towel still in her hands and the broken candle holder inside, she swung it at Brittany like soap in a sock, trying to make it hurt without causing injury. She struck Brittany's shoulders and arms, swinging fast enough that her foe couldn't get her hands on it.

She saw Lettie over Brittany's shoulder, her calm demeanor seeming sick in this situation. How could she be such a stone? Then a smile on Lettie's face made Madison frightened. Anything that made this woman happy couldn't be good.

Brittany cried out, "Stop it! Please! Stop!"

Madison stopped instantly, watching Brittany and trying to gauge if she was really surrendering.

"No more attacking, Brittany," said Madison. "I don't want to hurt you, but I swear I will if I have to." She heard laughter and turned sharply to the entryway where Lettie stood.

Lettie beheld Madison and Brittany, her head tilted to the side as if admiring a work of art. "The daughter of Iris Alexander. And now the granddaughter of Veronica Fedora?" she mused.

Startled, Madison stared at her.

"Oh yes," she said to Madison, "Brittany told me." She dropped a lit candle to the floor, a flame shooting up and running toward the pool.

A thrill ignited her eyes, as she cried, "It's Christmas!"

Chapter Thirteen

MADISON FLEW TO the entryway as Lettie stepped out and pulled on the heavy sliding door. Leaning her weight into it, Lettie slammed it shut and locked it a split second before Madison bounced painfully off the door, knocking herself half senseless. She staggered away a few feet, half bent over, clearing her head. Looking around the pool room, she took in the situation.

The nail polish remover with its acetone base had been a brilliant choice for a fast fuse. Lettie was able to set the fire from a safe distance and lock the door before Madison could stop her. The skinny running flame had instantly reached its target, igniting a patch of oil in the pool about two feet wide.

Across the way stood Brittany, confusion on her face. "Lettie? What are you doing?" she yelled.

Madison stared at the fire, trying to comprehend that someone could be that cold, that cruel. She saw that Lettie had parted the fluffy white curtains in the hallway. She had a perfect view of the pools. She lit a cigarette, watching the fire as it joined with another patch of oil in the pool. Flames leapt upward with enthusiasm, pouring smoke into the air.

Brittany screamed, backing up so fast that she hit the wall. It was what Madison needed to break her own spell of frozen fear.

She realized that the largest pool was the only one with the oil in it. Thankfully the pools were chemical free, so she wouldn't have to worry about chlorine gasses, but the toxicity from burning oil was plenty dangerous enough. They needed to get out. Fast.

She grabbed a few towels from the nearby table and ran at Brittany, shoving her away from the wall, wrapping her arms around her, and diving into the nearest of the smaller pools, taking Brittany with her. The water smacked her face and slapped her skin awake with bursting cold. They came up to the surface, gasping for air from the cold shock.

"Hurry," yelled Madison, grabbing Brittany's arm, yanking her toward the stair steps.

"Are you insane?" screamed Brittany, fighting off Madison's hands.

"That's my line. Now do as you're told and we might live through this!"

"I hate you," screamed Brittany, knocking Madison's hands away before bursting into tears. "We're going to die," she said, her terror growing by the second.

Madison slapped her hard in the face and shook her shoulders. "Listen! I had to get us wet before we run by that fire. We can get out of here but I need you, and you need me!" She pulled on Brittany's arm, dragging her toward the steps.

"Look," she pointed at the table of folded towels. "We can use the table to break the glass, but it'll take the two of us. We need a big enough hole to climb through. Our hands would never break through the glass in time, and we'd be sliced up trying."

The fire merged with yet another oil patch, and the clouds of smoke thickened.

Brittany's face showed her terror, and her hands covered her mouth, but she nodded. Madison climbed out of the pool, dragging Brittany behind her, splashing as her robe, heavy with water, weighed her down. Water poured off Madison's hair into her eyes and mouth. She sputtered out the water, wiping her eyes, but coughed on the growing smoke. She gave Brittany one of the towels that she'd been holding when they plunged into the water. Using the wet towel as a filter over her mouth, she ran past the fiery pool. The wavering flames licked at her wet robes as she ran past. Brittany followed, towel pressed firmly over her mouth.

As the waterfall poured into the pool, instead of helping to extinguish the fire, it had the effect of pushing the oil patches into each other. Where once there were peaceful blue waters, there were now flames undulating from the movement of the water, growing higher, joining flame to flame, their union increasing the hell.

Just when Madison thought it was frightening enough, the fire leapt to the waterfall. Madison had seen Lettie pouring the last gallon of cherry blossom oil all over its surface. Now that it ignited, the flames leapt higher into the waterfall tower, igniting the ferns and moss. The pool looked like a lake of fire with a flaming column at the end.

The sight propelled Madison forward to the trestle table, Brittany close behind her and clearly on board with the idea now. Together they did a table sweep with their arms, sending towels, robes, and vases of flowers crashing to the floor.

Madison tried to pick up her end of the table and was shocked to discover how heavy it truly was. Brittany had no better luck on her end. Unable to lift it, they scooted it across the floor, the thick wooden legs scraping angrily.

"Let's push one end of it to the glass wall, and we'll lift the other end up," shouted Madison.

Once they got the end of the long table within six feet of the glass wall, they combined their strength to lift the other end, standing the table up at an angle, supporting its heavy weight with their hands.

"Ready?" said Madison.

"Shut up and let's do it!" yelled Brittany.

With the table anchored on its end, their hands up high on its underside, they gave a forceful shove. The table rocked straight up and over, picking up speed as it plunged backward into the glass, shattering it with a loud crackling crunch. It landed on the gray rounded stones of the bottom half of the wall, giving a bounce before settling. The fire got a burst of energy from the extra oxygen flooding into the room and swelled in height and volume.

Coughing into her wet towel, Madison grabbed Brittany's arm, hauling her up the ramp that the underside of the table now formed. They ran the length of the table as if they were running on an uphill plank spanning the distance from the chamber of flames to safety on the other side of the broken glass. As they neared the top, with the white curtain forming a canopy at the end, the table teetered, acting like a seesaw, suddenly falling downward into the hallway, causing them to tumble the rest of the way, tangling into the frothy white curtains and landing in a heap together on the marble floor of the hallway.

Lettie was nowhere to be seen. Her partially smoked cigarette lay smoldering on the floor.

"Can you get a key to the front lobby door?" asked Madison.

Brittany nodded, her coughing subsiding.

"Then run there and call for help. No more faking it, Brittany. Lettie is not your friend. She wants us both dead, and we're going to need help."

"Where are you going?" said Brittany.

"Just go and get help," yelled Madison as she ran down the hallway, back to where she'd left Jason. She didn't know if she could trust Brittany enough to do the right thing where Jason was concerned.

It was one thing to leave him tucked away in a safe spot while she snuck out and called for medical help, but now there was a real fire spreading. She couldn't leave him back there half senseless.

As she ran, she was stunned at how quickly the smoke was spreading. It wasn't nearly as choking as it had been in the pool area, but she knew that would change fast. She wondered if Jason could run if she stayed by his side, supporting some of his weight and guiding him. And surely she'd be able to find another way out? Perhaps by the staff door that she'd seen Frank leave through earlier. Maybe Jason could recover enough of his wits to tell her where the extra keys might be.

She ran through the doors to the wine bar lounge and tore through the curtained room in the back, once again navigating the wine bottles on the floor, stepping through the wet sticky wine and out through the back door. She turned up the hall in the direction of the supply room where she'd left him asleep.

"Jason? We have to hurry, there's a fire and…" He wasn't in the corner behind the boxes. "Jason?" She whipped her head around. He wasn't in there. She stepped out into the hall.

"Jason? Talk to me. Try! I need to find you fast." Her voice faltered as she fought down her panic.

Then she got a whiff of smoke, but it smelled wrong. It wasn't the burning cherry blossom oil that she expected. It was cigarette smoke. She looked across the darkened hall and saw the glow of a cigarette in the distance. It was down low, indicating that the smoker was sitting.

She walked in the direction of the glowing embers, her feet growing heavy, wondering why Lettie hadn't left. She could've gotten away before any authorities showed up.

"It was too good to be true," Lettie told her, still some distance off. "Killing that sick little bitch to break her mama's heart… like she broke mine."

Madison eased closer.

"Then the most wonderful thing happened," said Lettie. "You showed up out of the blue. The granddaughter of the woman who caught my son and gave him to Iris." She paused, and then added, "Iris sent him to his death." She'd said the word 'death' like she'd deflated with it, her voice fading along with her will to rally.

"It's not right," whispered Lettie, as Madison came to stand in front of her. Jason leaned on the side of her chair, sitting up but asleep. The cigarette light glinted off the side of a knife blade she held near Jason's sleepy head. "While Iris and Veronica pamper themselves here in the spa, and pat themselves on the back for catching my son in his moment of weakness, my poor baby is cold in his grave." She sighed. "Life isn't fair."

Madison watched the burning tip of the cigarette rise, as Lettie brought it to her lips. The embers brightened as she took a pull, the heat intensifying with the delicate snapping sound of tobacco igniting. The glow illuminated her tired face, and Madison saw Lettie's eyes looking down at Jason. He raised his head, his eyes heavy lidded. He was still in bad shape.

"Lettie, please," Madison began. "I'm so deeply sorry for your loss. I can't imagine… there aren't words that can express… but nothing good can come out of this."

"Nothing good?" said Lettie, chuckling. "Of course not. It's not supposed to be good. It's supposed to hurt like hell. I want them to know what it's like."

"But spreading the pain isn't—"

"And I want my son back."

"—going to do you any…" Madison stopped at the sadness of her comment. "Of course you do. I wish I could give him back to you. But no one can do that and—"

"You heard me," said Lettie. "I want my son back."

"We would all want that if it were possible, but—"

"And this might bring him back. If the right people die, he can come back and get on with his life. He had so many plans. Did you know he was a beautiful pianist?"

In the silence of this confusing exchange, Madison realized Lettie was asking a sincere question. "Uh… no, I didn't know."

Lettie sighed. "He was so talented. He deserves a chance to pursue that. He chose to go into business instead… the lure of money, you know. But he'll be able to pursue his art this time."

"Oh, Lettie," said Madison, her heart breaking. When someone was that far gone, was there really a chance to get through to them? She thought not. But she had to try.

"*They* didn't kill him, Lettie," said Madison. "You know that. He was killed in prison."

"He wouldn't have been in prison," she said, "if Veronica hadn't caught him and Iris hadn't pressed charges. He would still be here today. He deserves a second chance."

"Of course he does," said Madison. "But I'm sure no one anticipated that he would be killed in prison. Someone in the prison did it, Lettie. Not my grandmother, and not Iris."

"Do you want a cigarette?" asked Lettie.

Madison paused for a moment. "Are you changing the subject because you know I'm right?"

"No, dear. I was offering you a cigarette. That's all."

Why this felt like a trick, she didn't know, but she didn't want to antagonize Lettie. "No thank you," she said politely, trying to keep her voice from shaking. "I don't smoke."

A silence followed, and Madison grew more fearful that she wasn't getting through enough to at least buy time.

"Lettie, would you let me trade places with Jason? Wouldn't that make more sense?"

Lettie blew out cigarette smoke. "You actually care about him that much? I think Brittany just wanted to be able to say she had a boyfriend. She would never put him in front of her own needs."

"I'm not Brittany," said Madison.

Lettie huffed. "Thank god for that. It took all the control I had to not strangle her every day while I waited for Frank to finally leave the spa for a few hours." She took another drag off the cigarette. "That, and keep him from speaking to Iris about her. It wouldn't have worked if she'd been fired." She laughed. "Although, it didn't work anyway, did it?"

"How had you planned to get away with it?"

"I didn't. Iris has blood on her hands and I want the whole world to know."

A few minor points fell together for Madison. "The red hand prints on the glass wall…"

"And the white lilies from my son's funeral. I threw them in the pool, yes." Lettie looked closely at the burning tip of her cigarette. "How melodramatic of me."

"I'll take that cigarette now."

It was Lettie's turn to pause. "I thought you didn't smoke."

"I don't, or rather, I haven't before. But I'm a little edgy and… I've heard it's relaxing."

"It's a bad habit. Shortens your life." She chuckled. "What poor timing on my part to think of that now."

"Would you light it for me?"

"No," she said, looking down at Jason and the knife in her hand. "My hands are a little full. It's not hard. You should learn." She shifted, presumably to draw out her cigarette pack.

Madison used the unguarded moment to lunge at her.

She grabbed the hand that held the knife, pushing it away from Jason, away from herself. She tried to get it away from Lettie, but the woman's grip was iron, her desperation giving her unusual strength. She seemed to think that her actions might bring her son back, so of course she would hang on as if his life depended on it.

The chair toppled back and the cigarette flew into the air, the momentum throwing their bodies backward and onto the floor. The sound of sirens grew in the distance, their wail slowing down as if arriving right outside.

"Little bitch!" Lettie screamed.

In the struggle, Madison didn't know where Jason was. One moment he was sitting at Lettie's feet, the next he seemed to be gone. In the dark, he could be anywhere.

As they rolled on the floor, Madison clamped both of her hands around Lettie's wrist. The knife in Lettie's hand pointed at Madison's face. It was one of the more frightening moments Madison had ever experienced, but it was about to get even more frightening…

… when the lights came back on.

The sharp tip of the gleaming blade inches from her face gave Madison a burst of terror that brought a surge of strength with it. She cried wordlessly as she twisted her body away from the knife, too frightened to let go. Lettie grabbed the weapon with her other hand, and now four hands pushed the knife in erratic swoops and dives.

Madison locked her elbows with her arms straight, and managed to get on her feet. Before Lettie could get on her feet as well, Madison quit pushing the knife away, and gave into Lettie's momentum. Pulling at the knife, she backed away, her butt leading, hoping that she was backing away faster than Lettie could come forward. She knew she must look ludicrous, but she didn't care as long as she was able to control the knife more than Lettie could.

Bent over, hanging onto the wrist that clutched the knife, she backed up at hyper speed, noting how difficult it was to run backwards when you're bent over. Lettie struggled to get her feet under her but was mostly dragged forward on her stomach.

It may not be in the manual for how to have a knife fight, but it would have to do for now.

She backed herself all the way through the curtains, back onto the marble tiled hallway under the bright lights. Then she stepped on something slippery, a spilled glass of wine from a panicked patron who vacated the building. She lost her footing and went down, her hands slipping from Lettie's wrist.

Lettie grabbed the opportunity, both hands still around the hilt. With a lightning fast upswing, she was about to plunge the knife down when the sweet shot of a gun rang out.

Madison flinched, just as she had at the gun range. She knew instantly who made the shot. Or at least, one of two possibilities.

The knife flew out of Lettie's hands, tumbling through the air to land several feet away, tinkling metal on marble as it skittered across the floor.

Nika, Ann, and Spenser ran up, Spenser falling to her knees next to Madison, eyes and hands quickly examining her for knife wounds.

Ann pulled Lettie's hands behind her back, while Nika stood nearby, gun still in her grasp, admiring the spot where the blood from Lettie's hand was spattered all over the floor.

Satisfied that Madison was intact, Spenser exhaled and held her close.

Nika observed, "I have never seen beautiful floor like this. Look how blood coordinates." She pointed at the tiles. "I wish this floor were everywhere I had to shoot someone."

Ann, Spenser, and Madison turned their eyes to her.

"What?" she said.

Chapter Fourteen

It was getting on to twilight in the parking lot. The blanket that the fire fighters had offered Madison sat on the hood of the police car she leaned against, still neatly folded. Autumn was around the corner in Seattle, but it was still warm enough that she didn't need the blanket, although she was sick of wearing the stupid robe. It had seen a lot of action that day, and displayed all the stains and dirt to prove it.

She sipped on a paper cup of coffee that someone had put in her hands, then dug around in a pocket, finding the small jar of mud. Somehow, through all the chaos, it had never fallen out. She also found broken pieces of pottery in there from her fight with Brittany and the vase. The other pocket had what looked like a piece of the moldy cake she'd accidentally grabbed in the dark and whipped off her hand. *Ew!*

The outside of the robe bore wine stains from when she'd found Jason on the floor and knelt down next to him. The red stains hadn't come out after diving into the cold pool with Brittany, and the robe was still wet enough to pick up every possible piece of dirt and every dust bunny when she rolled on the floor with Lettie in the back hallways.

Oh brother, I wonder what my hair looks like. She pushed it away from her face, but without some warm water and shampoo, she wouldn't be able to do much about it.

She looked behind herself, pulling at the fabric of the robe to see her derriere. Yup. There was fresh wine on her butt from when she'd slipped in spilled wine on the marbled tiles. If Nika hadn't been the excellent shot that she was… Madison shuddered to imagine what could've happened, the image of that knife about to plunge into her still fresh in her mind.

As a little girl she'd wanted an action-packed life, but this wasn't what she'd had in mind.

Her wonderful pedicure and manicure were now ruined, and she felt stupid that such a shallow disappointment could be so… disappointing. She'd weathered it all, taking each emergency as best she could. But as she stood there taking stock, finding a broken nail felt like the last straw. Her stiff upper lip was no longer stiff, and she wanted her mommy. Except that Ann didn't seem to be the kind of mommy that would understand a big pout over vanity. The girly-girl gene must've skipped a generation, because Nika seemed to have it.

Where are they anyway? Getting dressed?

The police had questioned her extensively about the events leading up to Brittany's escape from the building, as well as her confrontation with Lettie in the hallway. There'd been little time for Madison to get dressed in the locker room inside The Lazy Petal, though they were talking like they would let her do that pretty soon. Most patrons had already been allowed back in to get to their lockers, the fire having mostly done smoke damage in the hallways before being put out. The doors to the locker room had remained shut, so the room was still relatively clean.

Madison was tired and hungry as she leaned against the patrol car, but she couldn't even think about food until she knew what had become of Jason. They'd kept promising her they'd find out and get back to her.

A police officer pushed through the crowd, and people parted to let him past as he walked up to Madison. "I think we found your boyfriend, Ms. Cruz." His eyes were downcast.

"What's wrong?" she asked. "I don't like the look on your face." Panic rose in her gut all over again.

"Well, I just don't like to be the one who delivers this kind of news," he said.

"What is it? Is he okay?"

"He's just like you said. Confused, groggy. He seems to come and go, and he can't retain details of conversations that are taking place right now, let alone the details of the last few hours. The medics looked him over. He has a pretty bad concussion. They've already taken him to the hospital for observation."

"Where's he been? Was he asleep somewhere like I thought?"

"Turns out he's been out here in the parking lot the whole time."

"Then why couldn't you find him?"

He put both hands on his hips. "Well, first off, he doesn't have the presence of mind to understand that anyone was looking for him, or even that he's in need of medical help. One of the fellas finally figured it out when he noticed this tall guy in a black uniform shirt with wine all over his pants, like he'd been sitting in it. Poor guy didn't know anything was wrong."

"This all sounds exactly like I described to you."

"Yes, ma'am, you did," said the police officer. He clamped his mouth shut as he shook his head. Was he trying to hold back a smile? His manner indicated that he might as well say it and get it over with.

"So what did you mean that you hate delivering this kind of news?"

"All right… the other reason we didn't notice him right away is because while we were searching inside the spa for him, he was in the middle of all those ladies congregating in the parking lot. He became kind of popular out there, a big hit as a sleepy flirt. He's been hittin' on all the ladies, and instead of getting upset with him, they seem to think he's kind of cute in a puppy sort of way."

"I see," said Madison.

"Especially the older gals. I think he made their day."

Madison wanted to cover her face. She'd rather the cop think she had a problem boyfriend than tell him—or tell anyone except Jason's doctor—about Jason's overly amorous behavior in the back hallways.

His smile was no longer hidden. "But I wanted to add one more thing so you won't be too hard on him."

"You have the wrong impression," she said. "I have no claims on him. We've only been dating a few weeks, so… he's free to do whatever he wants."

"Still, I think you should know that he can't seem to keep anyone's name straight. Tells them all how beautiful and smart they are. And he calls all of them Madison."

✧ ✧ ✧

IRIS'S EYES WERE pink, as if she'd been crying. She came up to Madison and took her hand, patting it. "I don't know what to say. I'm so sorry my daughter acted the way she did."

"Oh Iris, don't," said Madison. "It's all right—"

"I hope you understand, she's not like that on her medication."

"I assumed it was something like that."

"If you hadn't been there, I would've lost her," she said, hugging Madison. "Thank you."

Spenser walked up and Madison made an introduction. Iris still seemed embarrassed this whole thing had happened and excused herself quickly. Madison didn't know how the law handled people like Brittany, but she knew that Iris would do whatever it took to help her. She also didn't know what would happen to Lettie, but it was clear that she was just as disturbed as Iris's daughter. She just hid it better. Hopefully they would both be getting help. But for now, just knowing they were in custody was a relief.

"The reason I came to find you," said Spenser, "is because they said you can go to the locker room now."

"Yes!" said Madison, bouncing on her toes. "I'm dying to get out of this thing."

"I decided to wait for you, so we can both go," she said, still wearing her robe too. "Solidarity, and all that."

"My own clothes will feel like heaven after all this."

"And if you miss having wine stains," said Spenser, "we can arrange to make a few on ourselves tonight."

"Personalized wine stains?"

"The best kind to wear."

"That's starting to sound like a plan."

"So much better than some random wine puddle you found on the floor somewhere."

They hurried across the parking lot, Madison's spirits lifting, eager for the locker room inside, till she heard a man's voice.

"Madison!"

She turned. It was Frank.

"Wait up," he called.

Her spirits did an about-face, retreating to the place where her ruined manicure now resided. *I'm too tired for this. I just want this day to be* over.

She watched as he trotted across the parking lot to where she stood. Dreading the next few moments, she reached for Spenser's hand to have something to hang on to, wondering if he would be looking for a way to blame the day's events on her.

"I'm glad you're still here," he said as he approached. "What a terrible thing to happen to you. And I'm sorry all this stuff had to happen on the one day you decided to try The Lazy Petal." He smirked, adding, "It's almost as if trouble follows you."

She didn't want to respond. She just wanted him to get it out of his system and let her get on her way. When her only response was squeezing Spenser's hand, he said, "Sorry. Too soon? I guess I shouldn't go trying to find the humor until I've apologized to you first."

"Apologized?"

"Don't make me spell it out," he pleaded. Madison watched him, genuinely confused. "Okay," he said, "I guess I will." He looked all around the parking lot, everywhere but at Madison, his posture casual as if he were trying to appear relaxed, but it was clear he was uncomfortable. "I should've contacted you a long time ago to apologize for the way I acted that day on the set. I know you didn't do it on purpose, and if I blame anyone, I should blame the director. But at the time..." He looked down, his hand on the back of his neck. "I know my behavior was not appropriate. Phobias are hard to reason with. A part of your mind knows that everything is okay, but the other part is screaming that you're going to die."

Madison thought of her fear of heights and understood what he was talking about. But she still didn't trust where this conversation might go.

He took a big breath, and looked at her like she mattered. "I was dreading having to face you because I was so mortified by my own behavior that day, so I kept putting it off. Then I let so much time go by it was even worse and I was more embarrassed." He went back to staring at the ground. "Look," he said, "I'm sorry. I want to make it clear that I am responsible for the way I acted that day. It was not your fault. I know you know that. But I'm trying to tell you, that *I* know that." He exhaled, like it was big relief to say it. "Hell, it wasn't even the director's fault," he added. "I agreed to do that shot because I was trying to prove to myself that I could, and I felt fine in there until the release button wouldn't work.

The director thought I was taking my time. It was an accident." He looked at her again. "Okay?" he waited. "Can we be friends?"

Telling herself that this wasn't a joke, that it was safe to let her guard down, Madison let go of Spenser's hand and shook Frank's.

"Friends," she said. "Thank you, Frank." It was still sinking in. "I didn't know how good that would feel until you said it just now." She inhaled a good deep breath and let it out. "Wow," she said, glancing at Spenser and back at Frank. "That's a load off. Thank you!"

"I'm sorry I waited so long. Please forgive me for that too."

"You got it," she said, glancing at a few police officers as they passed by, reminding her of the current situation. "So… what happens now at The Lazy Petal?"

"Obviously, we're going to need some time to repair the smoke damage in the hallways, and the fire damage to the pool room," he said. "But Iris says she wants to get started right away."

"Madison?" another voice called.

This one she recognized. "Nika!" she called back, waving her grandmother over to them.

Already dressed, Nika stepped up in her usual flair. Wearing expensive jeans and silver sandals, a colorful summery top, her dark red hair lazy and sultry on her shoulders, she moved with the grace of a woman who knows how to run in high heels.

"You are keeping good looking man to yourself," she smiled, offering her hand to Frank who lifted it for a light kiss on her fingertips. "You are manager, yes?"

Madison hadn't seen Frank behave so formally before. Was it something he'd picked up to greet the affluent patrons of The Lazy Petal? *Get your lips off my grandmother's hand.*

"Uh, Frank," said Madison, "I'd like to introduce you to—"

"Veronica Fedora," said Frank. "I've heard so much about you."

Clearing her throat, Madison said "And... this is—"

"My granddaughter calls you Frank? This is nickname for Franklin?"

"Francis."

Madison did not like Nika's dangerous smile as she rolled his name out of her lips so slowly. "Francis."

But Frank did seem genuinely surprised at the introduction, saying, "From your lovely eyes, I knew immediately that you must be related. But surely not Madison's grandmother," he said. "You look much too young."

Leaping between them, Madison said, "Nika, thank goodness you're here." She put her arm around her, turning her toward the locker room. "I've been anxious to talk to you." She looked over her shoulder. "You'll excuse us, won't you, Frank? I have a tiny emergency and need to talk to my grandmother." She waved goodbye to him as she hurried off with Nika, followed by a snickering Spenser.

As they arrived inside the locker room, Nika asked, "Is everything all right, little Madison?" She put her hands on either side of Madison's face and kissed her forehead. "What is this emergency you spoke of?"

Madison held up a finger. "I broke a nail."

Chapter Fifteen

SITTING AT HIS hospital bedside, Madison tried to tell Jason that he had nothing to be embarrassed about. For one thing, few people knew about his unusual behavior. His doctor was bound by doctor/patient privilege, and all the women in the parking lot that evening didn't really know him since he'd only been the wine server at The Lazy Petal for a few days.

The truth was, she'd overheard the nurses annoyed with all the calls coming in from anonymous women, inquiring about his condition.

His doctor had assured him that although it was not the most common symptom, some patients do indeed get more amorous immediately after a concussion. Just like most of the other symptoms, it had already faded away as he healed. They'd kept him in the hospital for a few days for observation, and seeing no further cause for alarm, they were sending him home later that day to rest. He most likely would be fine in a few more days.

Madison wanted him to come to the Killer Pancake dinner she was having at her place next week. After events at The Lazy Petal, she'd decided to put off the dinner and give herself some time. Now that she'd had a few days to reflect, she was looking forward to the warmth of food, family, and friends in her humble apartment. She thought it'd be good for them all to see each other in relaxed circumstances.

"So will you come?" she asked.

"Sure," he said. "It'll be nice to be with people who were there. I won't have to feel so weird if I talk about it."

"We haven't been able to talk about anything else. We keep comparing notes, trying to make sense of it."

"It's one of those things I'll never know," he said, "but it'll probably haunt me now and then."

"What will?"

He looked into the distance. "Wondering if Brittany would've gone off her rocker if I hadn't lied about being with you."

"Listen," said Madison, taking his hand for emphasis. "Getting upset with you or me was only a small part of what drove Brittany's actions. The main thing that made her even crazier than usual was Lettie's influence. Think about it. If Brittany hadn't gone banana balls with you and me, and upset the plan, Lettie would've succeeded in killing her that night. The way it turned out, Brittany lived. We all did."

✧ ✧ ✧

SHE'D PULLED OUT a dusty old recipe from the back of the kitchen junk drawer, otherwise known as the common household black hole. Everything made its way to the kitchen junk drawer: screws, rubber bands, paper clips, melon ballers, broken egg timers, cellophane tape, and gum so old it was rock hard.

But for some reason, the only recipe in there was the one for Killer Pancakes. Madison didn't remember how it got in there, but she knew that when it was time to make Killer Pancakes, the black hole of the kitchen junk drawer was where she would find the recipe. The part about the pineapple rings was easy. No brainer. But the part about how much flour, and how many eggs or teaspoons of baking powder, well... she couldn't fit all that information in the same brain that held the name of her favorite lipstick (Drop the Mic), or the number of stairs it took to get to her second floor apartment (twenty-three), or the many lines she'd been required to memorize from a script (way too few). So she took comfort in knowing that the recipe for Killer Pancakes that she'd written to herself in her childhood nestled safely in the black hole junk drawer from hell.

She slid the grocery bags across the counter, closer to the cupboard where she put things. She didn't understand why Nika had felt the need to contribute so many grocery items to this evening's dinner. Maybe she wanted to make sure that some of her favorite items would be on the menu?

Looking through the little treasures in the big brown bag, she found mostly more of the same ingredients that she'd already purchased herself: eggs, milk, flour and the like.

Oh good. A pound of bacon! That was a good idea. She set up the coffee pot, and then wondered if she should've bought decaffeinated coffee instead. She was used to thinking of pancakes as something you have for breakfast, but strong coffee at dinner might not be what people wanted. She pulled more items from the bag and found a small bottle of quality whiskey at the bottom.

Ah ha! They'll have a choice. They can put whiskey in the coffee if they'd prefer a more cocktail experience with their breakfast-for-dinner.

A knock at the door told her that Spenser had arrived.

"You ready to feed an army?" asked Spenser as she came in carrying a large glass bowl covered with plastic wrap.

"What army?"

"I'm the army. I'm ready to eat enough pancakes to wear you out in the kitchen."

"What's in the bowl?" asked Madison.

"Fruit salad. It's my token salute to something healthy and low calorie." Madison smiled, and Spenser said, "I don't know what got into me."

"It was a good idea. Thanks." She tried to clear a spot on the counter, but after crowding the sack of flour, the carton of eggs, and the whiskey together, she gave up and made a face. "There's not enough room for it on the counter. Can you put it in the fridge?"

Spenser opened the fridge and stared. "I don't know how you stay so skinny and gorgeous. You eat even worse than I do." She found a spot where she could squeeze in the fruit salad by shoving aside the leftover Chinese cartons, pizza boxes, sack of tacos, half eaten cookie dough, and petrified French fries.

Madison rummaged through her pots and pans, making a racket. She pulled out the only skillet she owned. "You know the drill. You show up early, I put you to work." But Spenser had already helped herself to the linen closet, pulling out an old used tablecloth with matching linen napkins that Madison had inherited from the grandmother that raised her, not the biological grandmother that she'd recently met. She wondered what Grandma Lisa would've thought of Nika if she were still alive. Strange how life marched on with new discoveries around the corner.

As the bacon sizzled and Madison measured out the batter ingredients, Spenser took down the plates, placing them around the table.

"Add a fifth place at the table," said Madison. "I asked Jason to join us."

"Really? I finally get to meet him?"

"Well, seeing him wander around The Lazy Petal parking lot doesn't count."

Spenser giggled. "I can assure you, he never hit on me, but I watched him hit on a lot of others. That boy's got moves."

Madison sighed. "He's *so* embarrassed." She tried not to laugh but couldn't help giggling. "Please don't let on that you saw him out there."

"Never," said Spenser. "As funny as it is, I really do want him to feel comfortable around us. If I got walloped on my head, I might run around doing embarrassing things, too."

"Like what, for instance?" said Madison.

"Oh, I don't know. I'm pretty proud of the tattoo on my tush. I might start showing it to everyone."

"I'm not stopping you."

"Don't tempt me." They laughed.

Another knock came at the door.

Nika bustled in with her arms full—a square foot box supported on one hip, purse swinging from the other arm, and two bottles of champagne clutched at the neck together with car keys.

Setting everything down on the counter in the small kitchen, they'd pretty much hit full capacity with only three people. Spenser grabbed the forks and knives and gave them some relief by leaving the cooking area to continue setting the table that was set up out in the living room area.

Nika opened the box that looked like it had just come from a department store. She pulled out brand new champagne flutes, setting them down with a mild clink on the counter.

"Nika, what did you do?" asked Madison, her eyes wide at the sight of the beautiful crystal. Afraid of mishandling the glasses, she picked one up with extra care, holding it up to the light. She'd never had anything that gorgeous in her humble little kitchen.

"Do not be scared. They are good quality crystal. I will wash them before we use them."

Madison turned the flute, noting the way the light refracted and sparkled. "They're beautiful," she said.

"You approve?" asked Nika, smiling.

"Well… of course, I mean, they're gorgeous. But why did you bring them?"

"I wanted to offer something nice for tonight's dinner. I'll make mimosas as soon as everyone is here."

Jason arrived soon after, and Madison was pleased at how attentive Nika was, keeping him in the conversation as if they were old friends. Spenser behaved herself, too, and made no jokes at his expense.

The whole apartment was filling with delicious smells and crystal sounds, and soon they would eat.

"When's mom going to get here? Have you talked to her? We should eat soon."

Nika's face was pleasant but blank. Madison hadn't seen her like this before.

She studied Nika for a moment and said, "What?"

"What, what?" said Nika. When Madison only continued to look at her, Nika added, "That is American way of saying it, no?"

"You lost me. American way of saying what exactly?"

"When you say 'what' and I say 'what, what,' that means I am asking you to clarify your question."

"Okay, let me ask it this way," said Madison. "Is there something you're not telling me?"

Nika waved her hand in the air, laughing. "There are many things I do not say to you. Which of these things that I do not say are you asking about?"

"Huh?"

Spenser had been watching Nika, and now shot a look at Madison, her eyebrows raised. Something was definitely going on, but Madison couldn't get the gist of what it might be.

A knock at the door meant Ann had finally arrived. Keeping her eye on Nika, Madison attended the frying pan but watched as Nika opened the door.

Ann stepped in, accepting hugs from Nika. Spenser joined in and Jason stood up, offering a hand to shake. Ann looked amazing to Madison, with open toed high-heeled sandals showing she'd had yet another pedicure, with red toe nail polish this time. Her skirt wasn't tight, but it was definitely form-fitting in a current style. Ann turned and faced Madison, a smile and sparkle in her eyes, coming forward with her arms up to receive a hug.

She's wearing makeup. Oh my gosh! "Mom," she gushed, going in for the hug. "You're beautif—" Over Ann's shoulder, a man had stepped into the entryway as well, shaking hands with Jason, doing that slap on the shoulder that men do. It was Frank Bergman.

The guys' laughter and Spenser's squeals over Ann's shoes covered Madison's initial shock. Ann went from hugging Madison to hugging Spenser, and the multiple voices and clinking crystal as Nika handed out mimosas to everyone added to the cues that Madison was picking up, cues to calm the hell down and act like everything was normal.

"I'll be right back," she smiled, wiping her hands on a towel. She rushed into her bedroom and closed the door. She didn't understand what she was feeling. She'd swear it was fear, but that didn't make any sense. There was nothing to fear right now, yet her heart was pounding and her breathing was faster. She put her hand on her chest and looked in the mirror as if there were answers there to questions she couldn't even put words to yet. She concentrated on slowing down her breathing. *Deep breaths. That's it, deep breaths.*

Frank was a good man. She knew that. Check.

Ann deserved to look for happiness like anyone else. Check.

Nika had arranged this and obviously approved. She wanted to growl, but check.

So what was her problem?

A tap at the door, and Spenser came in. Madison looked at her and asked, "What's wrong with me?"

Spenser stepped up with Madison's mimosa, which looked suspiciously pale. There was a lot more champagne in it than orange juice. Handing it to her, Spenser said, "Let's forget the part about what might be wrong with you, because you're a loving, generous, excited-to-be-alive person. Then we'll skip right to the part about what you need to focus on."

Madison stood there still holding the crystal flute.

Spenser gently nudged Madison's hand, bringing the mimosa closer to her mouth. "Drink up."

Madison did, and felt the dueling bubbles in her throat.

With one hand on Madison's shoulder, Spenser looked her in the eye. "Focus on this. You're not going to lose her. It's as simple as that."

"No, it's not."

"Yes, it is."

"But I barely got her back."

"I know you did."

"She already had a busy life, and she's finally making room for me in it, and now she's making room for her own mother, and now she's... she's..."

"You're not going to lose her," said Spenser, again.

Tearing up, Madison felt her lip start to shake. "It's not like I want my mother around all the time. God, no! She drives me crazy sometimes."

"I've seen it."

"We don't agree on most things!"

"I know."

"But I'd like to know she's there."

"Perfectly normal."

"What if she gets all caught up with him? What if they start a life together? What if she has more children? She's still young enough you know, and—"

"Does she have reason to worry that you'll get caught up with Jason, or some other guy, or whatever is down the road for you, and as a result she'll lose you?"

"No," Madison admitted. "I understand what you're saying but..."

"You're not going to lose her."

Madison downed her mimosa and sniffed. Looking in the mirror, she wiped the tears that had escaped, sniffed again, and let out a long exhale.

"I'm not going to lose her."

Chapter Sixteen

How many pancakes can a person eat before they pop? Madison suspected that Spenser came the closest to finding out.

Dishes with smears of syrup, remnants of pancakes, bites of bacon, and pieces of fruit salad landed in the sink piece by piece with sticky silverware, each waiting its turn to be rinsed off before being loaded into the dishwasher. Madison felt like a queen to even have a dishwasher. Her last apartment didn't have one.

The crystal flutes were mysteriously missing any sign of orange juice rings on the bottom. The juice had been quickly abandoned in favor of straight champagne.

After fumbling the syrup bottle and spilling syrup all down her clothes, Madison excused herself to change and put her shirt to soak in the bathroom sink. Upon returning, she found Ann and Frank at the kitchen sink, splashing water and laughing, insisting on finishing the dishes. She hadn't seen her mother like this before. Noticing that Spenser was watching her out of the corner of her eye, she made a casual move to Spenser's side, and whispered, "Thanks again."

She still had the sensation of feeling betrayed by Nika, but she knew that it was just an emotion, and that in reality Nika had done no such thing. Introducing Ann to a nice man was not about Madison—it was about Ann. Madison knew that fact in her head, but she was still waiting for the emotions to catch up. All Nika had done was make an introduction and let nature take its course. It annoyed her that Nika seemed to know how Ann would respond better than Madison did. But she had to admit, she hadn't been thinking about her mother in that way, and Nika clearly had. When you pay attention, as Nika had done, you learned things about people. Little things like whether or not it was time to introduce them to someone. Someone who might make them smile.

As Jason and Spenser brought the last of the dishes to Ann and Frank, she went up to Nika and hugged her without saying anything. Nika acted like she understood and smiled at her, moving a strand of dark hair from Madison's cheek and putting it back where it belonged.

They sighed at the same time.

✧ ✧ ✧

"DO YOU SWEAR you don't remember what happened?" asked Madison.

With everyone else gone, she snuggled on the couch with Jason. He'd been pretty good about following doctor's orders, taking it easy, but his week of rest was finished. The doctor had released him back to a normal level of activity. Music to his ears, he'd told her. He was bored out of his mind.

"Pretty much," he said. "It's spotty at best, but when they tell me about the parking lot, I'm so embarrassed I want to hide."

"I guess I'm not allowed to hold you accountable then," said Madison, drinking from her flute, "but you made some interesting moves." She indulged herself with a wicked smile, thinking she could get a lot of mileage out of teasing him.

"Thank you."

"For what?"

His smile was smug. "For liking my moves." He reached for her flute but she pulled it away from him.

"I didn't say whether I liked them," she said, clicking the flute with her finger, causing it to ring.

"Well, did you, or didn't you?" he asked, taking her flute from her.

"You'll never know," she said, looking up into those hazel browns.

"Oh, but I do."

"You'd be guessing."

"I don't remember most of it," he said, leaning forward to pick up the champagne bottle from the floor. He refilled the flute with the last spoonful of champagne. "But I didn't say I don't remember *any* of it."

She smirked, asking, "Do you remember—"

"Yes," he said, cutting her off. He looked in her eyes, pinning her there with his gaze.

She took a moment. "You don't know what I was about to say."

"Are you kidding? You've got that look in your eye."

She watched him, confused. "I have a look?"

"When you're thinking about *that*, yes."

"I do not."

He set down the flute and leaned in.

She insisted. "I do not have a look when… I mean… you don't know what I'm thinking about."

He still came closer, pushing her down on the couch and brushing her lips, but not kissing them. He murmured, "Let's say I do, and let's say you believe me." He nuzzled her neck, finding a ticklish spot, making her scrunch her shoulder up and giggle.

"I'm calling your bluff. They told you that you were hitting on all the women, right? So I think you're trying this just to see where it'll go."

"Am I getting away with it?" His smile was sheepish.

"No. I see right through you." She laughed. "You don't remember a damn thing, and even if I had a 'look,' we haven't been together long enough for you to have ever seen it."

"I saw it."

"When?"

"It was dark," he went back to her neck, "but I could still see you," he whispered. He nibbled on her ear, exactly the way he did before. Her breathing deepened and his hands began to roam. She squirmed. He definitely had some moves. "I want to see that look again."

She did a poor job of pretending he wasn't getting to her. "This doesn't prove anything."

He stopped for a moment and looked her in the eye. "I choose Tiffany."

She froze. "What?" she said.

"You promised."

"Now wait a minute…"

"I did what you asked."

"You remember?"

"I was nice and quiet. I didn't know why you were asking that, but at the time I didn't care.

"But—"

"And in exchange, you promised you would—"

"—but I at least deserve to know… who the hell is Tiffany?"

"Honestly? I have no clue. I don't know any Tiffanys. Now if you don't mind, I'd like to finish what I started."

Mind? What is he waiting for?

He resumed with an eagerness that took her breath away.

Life is crazy, and she knew that if you looked too closely, you would always find a reason to worry and fret. They were at the start of a new relationship, with questions and answers that wouldn't be asked or answered tonight. Tonight they should celebrate that they'd come through all right.

She opened her eyes. "Okay, I confess. I do like your moves."

"There's that look again," he murmured. "That's what I'm talking about."

She had, after all, made a promise. Good girls kept their promises.

And damn it, Madison tried to be a good girl.

The End

Excerpt

Stiff Competition

Madison Cruz Mystery 3

© 2015 Fevered Publishing LLC
All Rights Reserved

Chapter One

"Happy birthday, Mr. President," sang Madison, as she rehearsed in her car. Pursing her lips, she gave a sultry roll of her shoulder. The champagne blond wig tickled her skin and she felt her dangling rhinestone earring swinging. She turned left into the driveway of an elegant restaurant, driving up the parking aisle as twilight settled in. Tipping her chin upward, heavy lidded in her best Marilyn Monroe imitation, she blew a silent kiss then finished, "Happy birthday to you."

Two lanky young men dashed out from behind a parked truck, running in front of her moving car.

She jammed on the brakes, clinging to the steering wheel as her body jerked forward to the short screech of brakes.

Wide-eyed and laughing, the one in the baggy sports jersey looked barely college-aged. He pushed his short-haired friend in a blue t-shirt, who didn't look much older. The short-haired guy laughed and tried to hold his sports jersey friend back before he ran past him, racing to the front doors of the restaurant. Lost in their rough-housing, neither of them ever noticed Madison's car. They disappeared inside the restaurant.

Slapping her hand over her heart, she collapsed backward into her seat. She took a deep breath and exhaled as she closed her green eyes, silently scolding herself for being too caught up in rehearsing her Marilyn character. For now she'd better just concentrate on being Madison Cruz and wait for her racing heart to slow down. She'd need time to compose herself and get back into character. Good thing she was early for the gig.

She drove around to the back, searching for the service entrance. When arriving for a singing telegram, or in this case, a singing telegram and roast, she preferred using the service door so the customers wouldn't see her until she made her grand entrance.

She parked, then checked her makeup in the visor mirror. "Mr. President, honey," she said in her breathy Marilyn voice. Making eyes in the mirror, she said "May I call you honey? I just love powerful men." She added a touch more red lipstick, pressing her lips together to smooth the color. She loved these corporate gigs because they tipped so well and she usually drummed up more gigs from it. Phil, her agent, would be pleased.

One last read of the jokes she was supposed to deliver during the roast portion of tonight's festivities, then she tucked the paper into her big black tote bag. Climbing out of the car, she felt the chill in the Fall air. Her white Marilyn halter dress left her bare shoulders and cleavage to fend for themselves. She put a warm loose hoodie on, hiked her tote bag up on her shoulder, and headed for the service door, her sexy high-heeled sandals clicking across the pavement.

At the service entrance, standing between big garbage dumpsters and a stack of empty pallets, she pressed a buzzer. Her toes were getting cold.

The door whipped open and a man in kitchen uniform froze as he stared at her. In his thirties, slightly balding, the man looked up and down her body, but without an ounce of appreciation. He looked left and right, covering the small back lot with his gaze before returning his attention to her. He dried his hands on his white apron. "What do you want?" he barked.

"I'm the actress they ordered for the corporate party," said Madison, handing him her card. "My name is Madison Cruz."

"What corporate party?"

"Eldun Industries. They're surprising their president tonight at his birthday party." She smiled, expecting understanding to dawn on his face.

"There's no corporate party here." He started to close the door.

Madison called out, "Wait."

He stopped and gave her a moment.

"May I speak with the management, please?" When there are problems, Phil says, always go straight to the top.

"I'm the sous chef. That's all the management you need and I have to get back to work."

"But I have an event order." She pulled the gig sheet from her tote bag, brandishing it at the sous chef. "See? Pluto's Restaurant. The party is to be held in the Ficus room."

His tension eased up but a new irritation replaced it. "Oh. That." He looked her up and down again with a new scrutiny. He exhaled and seemed resigned. "Wait here."

He slammed the door, leaving Madison standing in the darkening twilight. The chill had insinuated its way through her hoodie. Her toes felt like ice.

What the hell is his problem? she wondered. Pluto's was an expensive restaurant. You had to be prepared to spend a chunk of your paycheck there, so she'd have thought their sous chef would be a little more polite. She looked around at the back lot of the restaurant. It always amazed her how nice restaurants never thought to clean the backside. The small grubby back lot was deserted, and added to her sense of being out of place.

Finally the door opened and a different man in a suit and tie greeted her. "I'm so sorry to keep you waiting." The light from the hallway behind him shone through his thin brown hair. "I'm Michael, the manager here at Pluto's." He extended his hand.

Madison shook it. "Pleased to meet you, Michael, I'm Madison."

"Your hands are cold. Come in, come in." He pushed the door all the way open so she could walk past. "Please forgive Carl. His workload is heavier than usual and he has a lot on his mind."

She followed Michael through a narrow hallway that wound past a tiny employee break room, an office door labeled Manager, and through a side section of the kitchen. Heavenly smells, sizzling, and voices calling out menu items filled the kitchen. Every inch of space was in use.

Passing through, they finally stopped at a door at the end of the skinny hallway. Madison could hear muffled laughter coming from the other side of the door.

"The Ficus room is in here," said the manager. "The servers use this door for delivering orders or bussing tables. The customers use a different door that leads to the open restaurant area. For obvious reasons you must use this door for your entrance and exits. Pluto's is not accustomed to this sort of thing and the patrons mustn't see you. I'm sure you understand."

She didn't understand. There was nothing scandalous about seeing a Marilyn Monroe impersonator. Most restaurants loved to let the other patrons see the fun going on. "No problem," said Madison. "Is there somewhere I can leave my hoodie and tote bag? The only thing I'll be carrying is the script of jokes."

"Jokes?" Michael wrinkled his forehead.

"Yes, Eldun Industries is providing the music."

He shook his head and murmured, "Things have certainly changed since I was a young guy." He looked down the hall in thought. "All right. I can accommodate you in my office." She followed him back down the hall, through the kitchen, out to the other hallway, and into the small office they had passed earlier. It was filled with boxes, a messy desk, and a few chairs. A battery-operated plastic clock ticked on the wall.

She set her things on a chair, dug through the tote bag, and pulled out her roast script, then folded it into a small fan she could use as a prop. "Marilyn Monroe is supposed to be introduced as a special guest," she smiled. "My contact person is Betsy from HR. Can you let her know I'm ready?"

The manager blinked. "I doubt there's a Betsy in there, but I'll let them know you're here. They'll send someone for you." He started for the door, then stopped and added, "Please, no warm-up for the kitchen staff. It would be much too distracting."

Warm-up? What was he talking about? she wondered.

He turned and left.

✧ ✧ ✧

HER FIRST WARNING was the smell. Heavy beer odors and the sharp scent of whiskey hit her nose as she entered the room. A young man in a club-style dress shirt escorted her through the crowd. She stayed in character as Marilyn, smiling, waving in the air to wild applause and frat boy party screams as she crossed the floor. Heavy after-shave assaulted her nose as she passed a young guy wearing a dress shirt that still had fold lines from the store package. She rolled her shoulders in sync with her hips as she sashayed to the front of the room, winking at random faces as she passed. In her breathy Marilyn voice, she said, "Oh my! Oh my goodness!" A t-shirted hipster lowered his sunglasses to look her over.

"Over here, sugar!" a man's voice boomed, as she stopped, front and center at the head of the room. She placed her hands on her hips and threw her head back to shake her blond wig before bringing her chin down low, looking at them with sexy eyes. More applause and shouts; then the cheers died off and a hush slowly grew, all eyes on her.

Pointing into the crowd with her folded fan, she cooed, "Where is that darling little president man?" She giggled. "I'm looking for extra diamonds, ooh!" she said, adding a squeak at the end of the sentence. People always loved her Marilyn Monroe character, but something felt off tonight.

A voice from the back of the room shouted, "Take it off!" Applause started up again.

Ignoring the rude shout, she stayed in character. "Where's that handsome birthday boy?" she asked cutely, as an inner dread began to grow. She put one red nailed finger to her lips as she looked around, using a coy smile to hide her confusion.

She did not like what she saw. Not one bit.

Everyone in the room was male. Maybe twenty or so, drunk young men. Where were the women? Where were the corporate suits? Where were the Happy Birthday signs and decorations?

"What are you waiting for?" a gruff voice shouted.

A cute young guy stepped up and asked, "Did you forget your music? Give me a second, I'll hook you up. This'll be perfect."

Then her eyes fell on the two guys she'd almost hit in the parking lot, the one in a sports jersey and the blue t-shirt guy with short hair. Their drunken faces shone with adoration as they watched her every move.

Her fist crushed the script of roast jokes she'd folded into a fan. She was going to kill Phil.

"Hey!" A man snapped his fingers in front of her face. "You okay?"

She whipped her head toward him, her Marilyn character abandoned. "This isn't Eldun Industries—" Throbbing club music started up, slamming into her ears, adding to her frustration.

"What?" he asked.

Madison repeated, "Eldun Industries." She said, louder, "I was hired to—"

"Take it off, bitch!"

"Get started, or I'll do it for you!"

She looked into the crowd, her fear growing. "This is a mistake," she tried to say, looking left and right.

"We're sick of waiting!"

"Shut up and let the lady do it her way!"

She braced herself, uncertain which direction to flee, frantically looking for the kindest face she could find. She darted to the guys from the parking lot. They may be drunk but they looked friendly. Okay, maybe the wrong kind of friendly, but she needed allies, fast.

The skinny guy in the sports jersey looked at her with a sleepy smile. "You're beautiful," he slurred. He looked at his short-haired friend next him. "Jay, I'm in love."

She grabbed his arm and yanked him in the direction of the door, saying, "I want you."

Jay burst into laughter, as the surrounding men roared their approval.

"Me?" His smile was ecstatic as he looked around at the other guys, showing off his good fortune, his chin held high. Hoots and back slaps rose up in support, with catcalls and applause as they crossed the room together.

"Yeah, Cliffy! You fuckin' virgin, go for it!"

They'd almost made it to the door when a big guy stepped in front of them. Holding a glass of beer at waist level, he swayed, saying, "Wait a minute. We've been waiting for this all night. Where you going?"

"I have to deflower Cliffy, here," said Madison.

"You have to...what?" His slow blink showed no comprehension.

She turned Cliffy around to face her, putting him between her and the big guy. She looked into Cliffy's happy face as she patted his cheek gently. She said, "I'm so sorry."

Then she put her hands on his chest and her foot behind his ankle. She shoved hard.

The crash and the laughter were both spectacular as Cliffy piled into the big man. Together they collapsed backwards into the table of food and drinks. It gave her the split second she needed to reach the door.

But it also ignited a chase.

Madison ran down the back hallway to the sounds of their footfalls on the hollow wooden floor. Their shouts and laughter indicated they thought this was a harmless game; but she knew that games have the potential to get out of hand. There was *no way in hell* she would wait to see which way it went.

She flew through the kitchen door and slammed headlong into Carl. The box he carried popped out of his arms, and small orangey colored mushrooms flew up and rained down on her head and all over the counters and floor. Carl stumbled back, crashing into a rack of pans. The entire kitchen staff froze in horror, more concerned with the sous chef's reaction then the mess being made.

Only two of the guys had continued the chase all the way into the kitchen. Cliffy and Jay laughed so hard at Carl they could barely contain themselves. As they approached Madison she grabbed a wide knife from a nearby cutting table and aimed it in their direction.

"Whoa, whoa!" Jay looked genuinely confused. "We're just having fun here."

"She's just playing," said Cliffy. He smiled, his lids heavy. "You run fast."

"What the hell is this?" shouted Carl, as Michael rushed in, surveying the mess and small wreckage. He looked at Cliffy and Jay with steel. The boys sobered up fast and ducked their heads, apologizing, making a swift retreat from the kitchen.

"You should get rid of those clowns, Michael," growled Carl. "It's not worth it."

Michael nodded his head. "Yes, Chef."

"Don't call me that." He slammed the box down on the cutting table, and stormed out.

Breathing heavily, her knife shaking in her hands, Madison fought with her conflicting instinct to keep her weapon brandished till she felt completely safe, versus feeling like an ass to be threatening people who didn't know her and hadn't done anything to her.

✧ ✧ ✧

"PHIL, I SWEAR I'm going to do you bodily harm," said Madison into her phone, "if you don't listen to what I'm saying."

Her elbows on Michael's desk, she leaned her forehead into her hand. Her dark silky hair hung forward onto the desk. The champagne blond Marilyn wig lay nearby on the messy desktop. She took some comfort in knowing that the manager kept his desk the same way she kept her closet. Her wig almost looked natural nestled in amongst computer cables, invoices, coffee cups, maps, and candy wrappers.

"If they'd been sober I could've explained things," she insisted, her voice getting loud. "But the way it was, they scared me." She slapped the desktop, demanding, "How did this happen?" Her chair squeaked in indignation.

"I don't know!" he wailed into the phone. "Jen was supposed to go to Pluto's, not you. I must've mixed up the addresses, somehow."

"The manager's hiding me in his office," she said, "while he settles everything down." She couldn't believe the young men had been allowed to drink that much in such a nice restaurant. Most places would've cut them off before it got to that point.

Phil sounded frantic. "My phone hasn't stopped ringing over this debacle," he said in his Boston street accent. "Your gig is the last problem I have right now."

She sputtered, "Do you have any idea what I just went through? How can this be the last problem you have?"

"Think about it," he said in a panic. "What's worse than the disappointment of not getting the stripper you ordered?"

Madison couldn't imagine at first, then it dawned on her.

"That's right," he said. "What's worse, is getting a stripper you did *not* order."

"Don't tell me," she said.

"Jen showed up at the corporate party for Eldun Industries, the ones who ordered Marilyn Monroe. And, well…Jen did what Jen does. No partial peel for her, she likes to go all the way."

"Oh no…"

"They're going to sue the pants right off my ass! I'm having a cardiac incident over this."

"Oh, Phil!"

"I'd never knowingly do that to you, girl. And I sure as hell would never inflict Jen on an unsuspecting business crowd."

"They're mad over here, too. But so far it's aimed at Cliffy and Jay, the guys who chased me into the kitchen."

"I'm surprised Pluto's hasn't called me yet," said Phil. "I gotta line up a lawyer. You'd better get out of there fast."

Chapter Two

A QUICK TAP on the office door, and Michael came in carrying a bag. Madison immediately shut off her call with Phil, sitting up straight, trying to look pleasant.

"Are you all right?" he asked. His gaze traveled to the desktop. She snatched up her wig but knocked over an empty coffee cup.

"Sorry!" she said, quickly picking up the cup before any stray drops could touch the maps.

"No problem," he said, calmly pulling the maps away. "You look much nicer as a dark brunette."

"Thank you," she said, smoothing her hair down, thinking of how crazy it must look right now.

He cleared a spot on the desk, saying, "I brought you something by way of an apology."

She wondered, Did I hear him right?

"I packed some food for you," he said, setting an elegant Pluto's carry-out bag onto the desk. "In all the commotion you may not have eaten in a while. This is just an *amuse bouche* and an entree or two and some grilled sides with our house aioli, but I hope it conveys my apology."

She stood up from the squeaky chair, looking into the bag of take-home boxes. The aromas of the kitchen rose from the bag. "Wow," she said, instantly hungry. "You didn't have to do that."

"On the contrary, I wish I could do more to make up for your experience here tonight."

"That's so kind." She looked up at him. "And thank you for understanding about me crashing into the kitchen like that. I was just scared."

"All forgiven."

"But I wish you hadn't hurried me off so fast. I wanted to help clean the mess."

"Carl knows where everything goes," he said.

"At least it didn't look like I broke anything. All I saw were mushrooms flying," she chuckled.

He gave a small smile. "Let me know if there's anything else I can do," he said.

She decided to take Phil's advice and get out of there. "I, uh, I'd better get going," she said, putting the blond wig in her tote bag.

She picked up the carry-out food, thanked him, and left.

✧ ✧ ✧

SHE TOOK THE exit off the freeway, and got stuck at a traffic light. Tapping her fingertips on the steering wheel, she watched the traffic. She'd been putting together a story in her head of how tonight's fiasco went. She would say the evening went well; that the audience was charmed. They laughed and threw money. Okay, don't go overboard, she thought. Just say they were charmed.

She'd say that she's getting bored of the Marilyn character and was looking forward to bigger challenges. She had to sound upbeat about it.

Naturally, she didn't want her mother, Ann, to find out what had happened. Ann worried too much about Madison as it was. But there was someone else who would make an even bigger deal about it. She sighed.

She dared not let her boyfriend, Jason, find out.

The car behind her honked. The light had changed. She accelerated, heading to her apartment, and wondered if she should pull over and call him, or wait till she got home. He'd be disappointed to hear that, on top of losing the first half of the evening with her due to the gig, now she wasn't going to come over to his place afterward. But she truly was tired. With tonight's disappointment still fresh on her mind, she didn't want to have to keep her guard up about what happened at Pluto's. But if she told him the truth about what happened, they would argue.

She wanted to go home and wear sloppy PJs and slippers, then fall asleep to black and white movies. It drove him crazy the way she'd fall asleep with the TV still on, and not turn it off till she woke up in the middle of the night. He once told her he had tried to stay awake one night, curious to see how long it would take her to wake up and turn it off, but he fell asleep and never found out.

She pulled into the parking lot of her apartment complex, parked, then pulled out her phone. Staring at it in the dark, she realized this wasn't going to be the first time she would lie to him about what happened during a gig. The last time she lied, it was because it was actually an audition instead of a paying gig. He didn't like her going to auditions because she might actually get cast and then he'd see her less during rehearsals.

Exasperated, she let herself fall backward against the seat. This was getting ridiculous. She was falling into habits that weren't good for either of them. It had to stop. As difficult as it was, she was going to have to tell him the truth, and he was going to have to deal with it.

It was too cold. She put the phone down while she sorted through her tote bag looking for her hoodie, but it wasn't there. She remembered wearing it when she first arrived at Pluto's. She must've left it in the manager's office.

She sighed. Well, maybe being cold would force her to make the call short.

"Hi," she said into the phone.

"Hey, Madness." After hearing Madison's mother call her Madness, he agreed the nickname fit. He'd been using it ever since. "Where are you?" asked Jason. "Is that corporate party over?"

"Yeah, it's... that's not why I'm calling actually." She swallowed. She'd give him the details of the gig later. "I hate to disappoint you but I think I'd rather just stay home tonight. I'm so tired and I just want to fall asleep watching TV. Would you be all right with that?" She braced herself, but he surprised her.

He sighed. "Sure. I understand. I guess even singing happy birthday can wear a person out, huh?" he chuckled.

She resisted the urge to explain how so much more went into being a singing telegram than merely singing happy birthday. But she decided to accept his gracious response. "I'm...glad you understand. I'm going to eat something, watch TV, and pass out. It'll be glorious for me, boring for you."

He laughed. "No problem. I'll pick you up tomorrow and we'll get some lunch. I found this great little place—"

"I'm doing lunch with Spenser and Target tomorrow, remember? We've been planning this afternoon together for weeks."

He was silent for a moment. "Tomorrow's my only day off this week."

"I know, but we agreed on this."

"That was before you accepted the gig with the corporate party. You'd rather sing happy birthday than be with me."

"It's my job! I have bills to pay."

"And as a result you're too tired to come over tonight."

She scrambled to find words. "Look..." She felt accused, but of what? It pissed her off. She took a breath, wanting out of this conversation. "I'm sorry, Jason. I didn't plan it to go this way, but I'll still see you tomorrow night. I'll spend the afternoon with Spenser and Target, then I'll meet you for—"

"I don't understand how you live with the chaos of your job. We can never plan anything."

The car was getting colder. She pulled her arms inward to hug her body. "Jason, I see you every other day, at the very least. We have jobs, friends, family...lots of things can come up. It's natural."

He sighed again. "I don't want to get into this now. You get some sleep and we'll talk later. All right?"

She had the sense that she was being handled as if she were the problem. But she agreed with one thing. She didn't want to talk about it either.

After ending the call she made sure she had everything in her tote so she could make a quick run to her apartment.

Just then, she heard a familiar sound, a loud distinctive metal crunch, meaning someone was throwing out garbage. The landlord should fix the lid to the garbage bin, she thought. It sounded like a car accident every time people took out their garbage.

Getting out of her car, she hiked her tote bag onto her shoulder and grabbed the Pluto's take-home boxes. Yum. She couldn't wait to dig into those.

Cold and hungry, she hurried across the parking lot. Maybe this night wouldn't be a total loss after all. She got excited at the thought of fuzzy slippers, black and white movies, food from Pluto's....

The sound of a woman crying brought her up short. She stopped and looked around. A figure stood in the dark near the garbage bin.

Madison sighed. This was one of those moments when she had to make a judgment call. Did this woman need help, or did she need privacy? Should Madison mind her own business and go inside where it was warm? She waited a second, hoping for another hint. After a moment, she called out, "Are you all right?"

The woman turned her head. Under the street light Madison recognized the new neighbor from downstairs, short and curvy, with brown hair pulled up into a sloppy knot. She guessed her neighbor was older than she. Maybe thirties.

"I'm Madison," she said, as she slowly approached the woman. "Your name's Vivian, right?"

Vivian nodded, quickly wiping her face and eyes. "I'm sorry," she said.

"Don't be sorry. If you'd rather have privacy you just tell me, but if you need help," Madison shrugged, "I'm here.

Vivian gave a short quiet laugh. "I'm an idiot. Normal people cry in their house. But not me." She lifted her arms and let them fall to her sides. "I have to cry outside."

Madison gave her a soft smile in response. "Hard night, huh?"

"You could say that." Vivian bent to pick up a sack, hefting it into the garbage bin. "I was fine till I had to throw out the garbage. It felt symbolic."

Madison adjusted the tote bag straps on her shoulder. "Of what?"

"My love life." Vivian closed the garbage bin. Its metallic slam and crunch made Madison wince. Vivian continued, "My ex-boyfriend came by earlier today. He smashed a few things just because he knew I liked them."

Madison barely knew this woman, but her heart broke for her. "Jerk," she said.

"Yeah. He's a jerk." Vivian sniffed, pulling a tissue from her jacket pocket and wiping her nose. "But you know what? It feels good to take out the garbage. Good riddance." She looked at Madison with concern. "You're shaking. Let's get inside the building."

"I'd love that," said Madison, grateful to get out of the cold.

Inside, as they walked along the hallway of the ground floor, Vivian shoved her tissue back into her jacket pocket. "Thanks for stopping to see how I am."

"I didn't know if you needed help or not," said Madison.

"I didn't know either. But I guess I simply needed someone to talk to," Vivian sighed. "It did help. It'll make the rest of it easier."

"What's the rest of it?"

"Cleaning the mess he made when I left for the store. I'll be up pretty late."

"He did it while you were gone?"

Vivian nodded. "He drives a red car. I've been seeing it around here a lot, and he knew exactly what to break. He must've been waiting for me to leave."

"How did he get in?"

"I'm not sure. I thought I'd locked the door but the windows look untouched."

Madison came to the stairwell that led to her apartment on the second floor as Vivian arrived at the door of her apartment.

With her hand on the rail, Madison looked back at Vivian. "Did I already mention he was a jerk?"

"I'm liking you more and more," said Vivian.

✧ ✧ ✧

LUXURY! STRUTTING AROUND in her fuzzy slippers and sloppy PJs, she wanted to hug every pillow in the house. She removed all her Marilyn makeup and gave her hair a vigorous brushing, which always felt good after a bout of wig wearing. Finding a small orangey mushroom in her cleavage when she removed her Marilyn costume was embarrassing, but she was pretty sure no one saw it. In spite of her trim figure, her cleavage was enough to hide more than one mushroom.

She cleared the couch of old gig sheets, mail, and laundry, then threw a cozy blanket down on it. Turning on her small television, she set it to an old movie channel, wondering what black and white delights awaited her. Grabbing her favorite pillow, she bounced it off her face a few times in a solitaire pillow fight before sailing it up and over to land on the couch. Tonight would be epic!

Entering her tiny kitchen, she kept an eye on the television from over the counter. Peeking inside the take home boxes that the manager of Pluto's had packed for her, she inspected each one. Hearing voices from the television, she turned to look. A woman had pulled a gun on a private eye, but he laughed. "You think I won't?" asked the woman. "I think you could," said the man. "That's what I like about you."

Madison plunged a fork into the first box. What the hell? Who ever heard of draping a sunny-side egg on top of asparagus? But when she ate the first bite, flavors burst like fireworks onto her tongue: char from the grill deepened the earthy asparagus flavor, while the fatty yolk balanced against the bitterness. A touch of stone ground mustard and a peppery hint of fresh arugula embraced a shred of sweet red bell pepper. She stared at the box in happy disbelief, and thought the whole fiasco of the gig tonight was almost worth it. This was profoundly delicious!

The movie voices went silent as the soundtrack music swelled. Madison turned to see the TV couple in a dramatic kiss. She sighed.

She suddenly had an idea that caused her mood to spike even higher on the happy meter. She decided to surprise Vivian with her bounty of Pluto's take home boxes. Vivian said she'd be up late anyway, and there was enough food here to feed three people. She figured Vivian could probably use the distraction. They would feast on fine cuisine!

She closed the boxes and put them back in the bag. She grabbed forks, spoons, and napkins and dropped them into the Pluto's bag, then headed out into the corridor. Downstairs, she knocked on Vivian's door.

Vivian opened the door looking tired and confused. She held the doorknob in one hand, a broom in the other.

Her eyes traveled over Madison's PJs and fuzzy slippers while she nodded, saying, "I love your wardrobe."

"I bring tidings of great joy." Madison held up the bag. "Or at least great scarfing. I've decided in my superior wisdom that you need to help me eat this. It's from Pluto's and it's so good you're going to die. We're both going to die with smiles."

Vivian blinked. "Uh..."

Madison lowered the bag. "Are you hungry?"

"Well..." Vivian exhaled with a rueful smile. "I'm always hungry. That's not the problem." She looked over her shoulder and back at Madison. "Come in. See for yourself."

Madison followed her into the apartment. Her eyes widened as she looked around. Vivian's apartment was the identical floor plan to her own apartment, but no one had come in and messed it up like this. This was sad.

Vivian closed the door behind her and said, "Uh, please excuse the mess?"

"Oh my God." Madison stared.

Vivian sighed, stretching her back. "I've picked up most of it, but I'm wearing out."

There were trash bags sitting nearby, no doubt waiting to be taken out. A dustpan filled with debris sat on the kitchen floor. Pieces of broken dishes were on the counters, but also in odd places like a desk or on a chair cushion, as if plates had been hurled against the wall to shatter in flying pieces. A white powder ran in a wide swath across the carpet and onto Vivian's couch. An empty flour bag nearby told what the white powder must be. A wooden chair on its side was missing a leg, which was wedged into the broken glass door of a bookcase. Tomatoes had been flung at the ceiling, leaving orangey splotches above them, while a sad iron lay on the counter, useless because its cord had been ripped off.

Madison gasped as the thoroughness of it sank in. "Vivian. You called the police, right?" She whirled and looked at Vivian's exhausted face.

Vivian turned away. "No. And please don't tell the landlord." She resumed sweeping in the kitchen.

"You should call the police!"

Vivian shook her head vigorously. "My standing with the landlord is delicate already." She looked at Madison. "My credit rating is bad but he took a chance on me. Russell knows that and he did this to get me kicked out." She gripped the broom handle. "I'm not going to let him win."

"The landlord wouldn't evict you just because you were vandalized," said Madison.

Bent over, Vivian carefully swept more tiny pieces into the dustpan. "No, but if he thinks I attract a bad element he might find a different excuse."

"But—"

"Please." Vivian stood up straight, pleading with her eyes. "I want to stay here."

Watching Vivian, Madison's own problems seemed to shrink. Uncertain of what to say, she finally put the Pluto's bag down and gave Vivian a hard hug.

"Promise me?" asked Vivian.

"I promise."

They broke the hug. "In fact," said Madison, "I'll help you fix it so the landlord will never know." She looked around. "Where should I start?

"Are you kidding?" Vivian leaned the broom against the kitchen counter. "I just had this crazy girl come to my door in her pajamas, offering to feed me. I'm not going to pass up that offer." She smiled and nodded at the bag. "Show me what you brought."

"Well," Madison started, "you'll never believe what—"

A metallic rattling at the doorknob interrupted them. In a tiny voice, Vivian said, "How did he get a key?" The fear in Vivian's eyes told Madison who it must be.

The door slammed open.

Watch for Stiff Competition

Coming soon!

We hope you've enjoyed this excerpt of Stiff Competition: Madison Cruz Mystery 3. Please look for this, and other works, by Lucy Carol.

About the Author

Lucy Carol's top priority is to entertain you, and keep you turning pages. She writes mysteries for those who like it fun, fast, and don't mind losing a little sleep. Living and writing in the Pacific Northwest, she loves martinis, flowers, dancing, a good lipstick, and cake. Her background is in the performing arts, having been an actress, voiceover artist, choreographer, and singing telegram.

LucyCarol.com

Connect with Lucy on Facebook

www.facebook.com/lucycarolbooks

Also by Lucy Carol

Hot Scheming Mess: Madison Cruz Mystery 1

Stiff Competition: Madison Cruz Mystery 3 *Coming soon!*

Thank you for reading!

Your honest review is more important than you may realize. Other readers value your opinion more than they value advertising. An advertisement can tell them that the book exists, but only you can tell them if you liked it! Thank you for your support!

Made in the USA
San Bernardino, CA
15 August 2015